I'll Be

HOME

for

CHRISTMAS

STRIPES PUBLISHING
An imprint of the Little Tiger Group
1 The Coda Centre, 189 Munster Road, London SW6 6AW

A paperback original
First published in Great Britain in 2016

ISBN: 978-1-84715-772-0

Printed and bound in the UK.

2 4 6 8 10 9 7 5 3 1

Holly
Bourne

Tom
Becker

Sita
Brahmachari

Kevin
Brooks

Melvin
Burgess

I'll Be

HOME

for

CHRISTMAS

Katy
Cannon

Cat
Clarke

Tracy
Darnton

Juno
Dawson

Marcus
Sedgwick

Julie
Mayhew

Non Pratt

Lisa
Williamson

Benjamin
Zephaniah

stripes

Contents

Introduction

Home means something different for everyone. Many of us are fortunate enough to count our home as a place of stability, love and safety; others are not so lucky. Fiction can be our first exploration of hardships that are very much part of the real world. By using fiction both as a means of raising money for Crisis and increasing awareness of the struggles faced by those who experience homelessness, this collection bridges the gap between the real and the imagined.

As part of the creation of this book, **Lisa Williamson** has generously donated her time to Crisis, giving a creative-writing workshop to members at the Crisis Skylight Centre in London. In turn, some of the Crisis members shared their stories with her. This exchange of ideas and experiences has in part formed the inspiration for Lisa's story, 'Routes and Wings'.

Stories of hardship and resilience are also the basis of **Benjamin Zephaniah**'s poem, 'Home and Away', and 'The Letter' from our competition winner, **Tracy Darnton** – a story that is powerful in its simplicity. 'Amir and George', a moving story from **Sita Brahmachari**, focuses on the experience of losing your home and coming to terms with a new one as a refugee, a situation that is tragically common in our world today.

Campaigns like Crisis at Christmas provide moments of hope in the face of adversity and this anthology is not without Christmas spirit. There are stories filled with the warmth of the festive season, from **Katy Cannon**'s 'Christmas, Take Two' to **Non Pratt**'s 'Ghosts of Christmas Past' and **Juno Dawson**'s 'Homo for Christmas'. In not one of these stories is happiness easily found, yet it is recognized as all the more precious when it arrives.

Other stories in the collection are far from cosy. **Melvin Burgess**'s 'When Daddy Comes Home' casts a sceptical look at politicians and truthfulness and **Marcus Sedgwick**'s 'If Only in My Dreams' presents us with the uncertain future of our planet. These are stories that will stay with you well beyond their final lines, as is **Tom Becker**'s chilling vision of the demons unleashed by grief in 'Claws'.

Yet even in the most difficult of circumstances and the most imperfect of homes, there are moments of beauty to be found. **Julie Mayhew**'s 'The Bluebird' sees a girl yearning for escape, **Kevin Brooks**'s 'The Associates' reveals tenderness in friendship and **Holly Bourne**'s 'The Afterschool Club' shows us that there is more to most people than there first appears.

In **Cat Clarke**'s story, 'Family You Choose', a group of self-confessed 'waifs and strays' are family for one another despite their differences, with heart-warming results. Here we present to you a family of sorts; a collection of wholly individual, beautifully written and thought-provoking stories, each one a member of the rich and varied family of UKYA writing. How fortunate we are.

Ruth Bennett, Commissioning Editor
Stripes Publishing – June 2016

A Note from the Publisher

In September this year, Stripes will celebrate its tenth birthday. We wanted to mark this important milestone in a meaningful and imaginative way. In publishing *I'll Be Home for Christmas* our aim is not only to provide crucial financial support to Crisis, but also to raise awareness of the charity's work among young adult readers, particularly at this time of year. Most of us take it for granted that we will share Christmas with family and friends, but for an alarmingly high number of young adults this isn't the case.

Stripes is primarily known for its illustrated fiction, so this has been an amazing opportunity for us to reach out to the YA community in the UK. We have got involved in some of the fantastic initiatives celebrating YA fiction, including the Young Adult Literature Convention (YALC) and *The Bookseller* YA Book Prize.

We also ran a competition to find a new voice in YA and are delighted to welcome Tracy Darnton to the anthology.

I am hugely grateful to all the exceptionally talented authors for their involvement in, and their commitment to, *I'll Be Home for Christmas*, and for their wonderful contributions – they have produced such a diverse and inspiring range of stories and poetry and each one has offered a unique response to the theme of home. We've eagerly awaited the arrival of each piece; some have made us laugh, some have made us cry – all have made us think...

And a massive thank you to William Grill for his stunning cover – it superbly captures the essence of the book and is the most delightful wrapping paper this Christmas anthology could have.

This has been a truly rewarding and exciting experience for all of us at Stripes – and a fantastic way to celebrate ten years of publishing. We go forwards into our next decade with renewed dedication and energy.

Jane Harris, Publisher
Stripes Publishing – June 2016

Home and Away

*

Benjamin Zephaniah

I'd like to be home for Christmas.
That's where the rhythm wise hip-hop is,
That's where the rock and the jazz is,
The place where I dream happy
Where I dance to sweet homemade reggae.

I'd like to be home for Christmas.
The world can be viewed from the back room,
It lights up in the soul full moon,
From there it's my stars that I see
There dwells the real history of me.

I'd like to be where my heart is.
Childhood naughtiness I can't defend,
Kids' arguments that never end,
We shout and fight so endlessly,
Apparently that's family.

I'd like to be where my toys are.
To hear the sounds of me back then,
To be ambitious and hope again,
To stay if I choose not to leave,
To hunker down, to chill, to breathe.

I left home one year – around Christmas.
I went off to do some big man things,
Me and mine we lived like kings,
My pad was smart, and safe, and lush,
Yes, we were ghetto fabulous.

But it all fell apart – around Christmas.
My safety net just up and went,
No insurance, no friends, no rent,
My descent was hard, painful and short,
And me – too macho to seek support.

I lost my way – around Christmas.
I suffered alone in many a crowd,
I begged where begging was not allowed,
I cried and prayed, but no one heard,
No god or statesman said a word.

I could not celebrate last Christmas.
The angry cold took hold of me,
The vermin would not leave me be,
And richer folk blamed me for crimes,
Inside my pride died many times.

So I'd like to be home for Christmas.
But now I am a refugee,
My family has disowned me,
Depression came and made me low,
I found me with no place to go.

We can't all be happy at Christmas.
Civilization, humankind,
Can I get some peace of mind?
Turn your body, shift your eye,
The great and good just pass me by.

What makes a home at Christmas?
Is it he who offers me a smile?
Or she that stops to talk a while?
Some spare cash in an envelope?
Or they that stop and offer hope?

Crisis will be home for Christmas.
Compassion came and rescued me,
Advice with heart and empathy,
Touched me with a helping hand,
Now I have a better Christmas planned.

Ghosts of Christmas Past

*

Non Pratt

I walked past our house today. It's the first time I've seen it without a sign outside – FOR SALE – UNDER OFFER – SOLD. Somehow seeing it without any sign at all is worse, like the house is waiting for me to walk up the drive and in through the front door.

But I'm walking through a different door now. Late.

"Where've you been?" Nan says when I walk through to the kitchen, where she and Theo are.

"Nowhere."

She tuts. "You've obviously been somewhere, Samuel, or you'd have ceased to exist."

Reckon she'd prefer that – always on about my 'enormous' shoes cluttering up the porch, how much food I eat, why there are so many of my clothes in the wash. Doesn't help having ten-year-old Theo around being small and unsweaty and not having to watch his blood sugar because he's not the one with diabetes.

I peer over his shoulder at his homework and point to one of the answers.

"That's wrong," I say, because I know how much he hates it.

"No, it's not!" But he huddles over his workbook to hide the fact he's correcting it.

"Leave your brother alone." Nan hands me a plate of browned apple slices arranged in a wheel around a single oatcake that she's taken from the fridge. I guess it's good that she's watching out for me, but it's hard to feel grateful when she grumbles about what a faff it is and tells me off for helping my brother with his homework.

I take my sad little snack up to the bedroom because it's the only time I get the space to myself. Not that it feels that way with Theo's inside-out jeans on the floor, socks still bunched in the leg holes, and his stuff charging in every socket. I can't even shut the door because of his rucksack hanging on the handle.

Getting my phone out, I catch up with Bazza about the party plans for Friday while googling tips on how to talk to girls. I'm none the wiser when there's a knock on the door and Mum pokes her head in. I hadn't even heard her come back.

"How come you're skulking up here?" She sits on Theo's bed.

"Doing Nan a favour by staying out of the way."

"Stop being daft," Mum says.

"I'm not! She's always tutting about me leaving stuff in the wrong place, keeps wanting to know where I am or what I'm doing. Like she thinks I'm out dealing drugs or doing knife crime unless I'm sat next to her on the sofa watching *Countdown* and doing a jigsaw."

"I don't even know where to begin with that!" Mum's expression wavers between annoyed and amused. "It's perfectly reasonable for her to want to know where you are – and what's all this nonsense about drugs and knives? *And*, since we're talking clichés, my mother has never watched *Countdown* or shown any interest in jigsaws."

"Maybe not, but she doesn't have to tell me off every time I leave the bread on the side."

"Stop leaving it on the side, then!"

"Yeah, but, what kind of psychopath keeps bread in the fridge?"

"The kind of psychopath who puts up with having an ungrateful scrote like you around." Mum stands up as if to go, reaching out too fast for me to escape as she ruffles my hair. "Come down and lay the table for tea, scrote."

*

On Friday I walk with Bazza back to his, my bag loaded with clothes to see me through tonight and on to lunch with my dad and Theo tomorrow. When we pass my old house I notice there's still no wreath on the knocker, no fairy lights wrapped round the columns by the door or looped in the holly bush. No sign that anyone is looking forward to Christmas the way we all used to.

Makes me think they don't deserve it.

It's something I can't get out of my head, a rut my mood gets stuck in. Hours later, even with the party up and running, all I do is drift round not quite clicking with anyone. In the lounge, I sip my watered-down orange juice and watch some girls perform an impromptu karaoke to 'All I Want for Christmas'.

"Best Christmas tune ever. Discuss."

There's a girl next to me who wasn't there a minute ago. She's wearing a spangly top, her hair braided in a loose side plait, a careful cat-flick lining her eyes.

"I – er…" I manage.

"I know 'Fairytale of New York' is cooler, but I always think Christmas is for cheese." She's got a Scottish accent and although I've seen her around school, she only started after half-term and I don't know her name.

"Cheese works for me," I say, then there's a long pause before I add, "I'm Sam. Wright." Because I don't want her to confuse me with Sam Bastian who is gay. I've enough obstacles to overcome without girls thinking I prefer guys.

"Amy Sparrow," she says.

Neither of us know what to say next and I go with a desperate, "So – er – how are you liking St David's?"

"It'll do. For a school." Amy does that thing where you nod along with your words as if that makes them last longer.

"Made friends?"

"A few…" She scans the room as if looking for examples. "Thought they'd be here, actually, but…"

More silence – lots of it.

"OK, so," Amy says a little too brightly, "it was nice to meet you, but I've got to..." She gestures out of the door and before I have a chance to respond, she's gone.

All that googling and I still don't know how to talk to girls.

I decide to take a break and go out front, appreciating the way the door clunks shut to mute the party behind. Cold air laps at my skin and even though the step is bum-numblingly cold, the dull ache of it is weirdly comforting as I sit and stare out into the night.

The houses here are older and smaller, closer together and harder to tell apart than where I used to live. It doesn't feel great to admit I pitied Bazza for living in one – doesn't feel any better admitting I envy him for it now, living close to school with both his parents and a bedroom all to himself.

There's a swoosh behind me and someone nearly trips over me on their way out of the house. I leap up as they right themselves by grabbing at a festive hanging basket and I recognize Amy Sparrow's scruffy plait and sharply lined eyes, above a scarf so chunky it covers half her face.

"Oh, it's you," she says. "Hello."

"Hi."

"And also goodbye."

"You're leaving?"

"No, I've yet to grasp the English language and don't know what I'm saying." She sounds more Scottish than ever. "Yes, I'm leaving. Nice meeting you, Sam Wright."

Regret nibbles at my insides. Even though our first contact bombed, I was hoping there'd be a second…

"Would you like me to walk you home or something?" I blurt out.

Amy turns back and, although I can't see her mouth, I know she's smiling. "You don't even know where I live."

"I don't have to know the way to keep you company."

As comebacks go, it isn't bad (for me) and she laughs. "I'll wait while you get your coat."

*

Like an idiot, I ask if she's from Scotland.

"Was it the flag painted on my forehead that gave it away?"

"Well, you hide your accent so well…" I try out her

brand of sarcasm and she seems to like it.

"You should hear my sister – she's at university in Dundee and jokes about how English I'm becoming."

"How is it, living here?"

"Weird." Amy kicks at a stick on the path. "It's not the place so much…"

"…As the people?" I guess and she grins.

"Just one – Greg."

"Boyfriend?" I feel a right tit the second I say it and Amy gives me a funny look.

"Not mine – Mum's."

Does that mean Amy *does* have a boyfriend? I hope not.

Amy keeps kicking the stick until it snaps, then she sighs. "I'm not being fair. Greg's all right – it's just weird living with someone I'm not used to."

"Does he keep bread in the fridge?"

"*What?*"

And then I have to explain it, don't I? Only somehow it doesn't end up being about Nan and the bread. It becomes Mum and Dad getting a divorce – them selling up and me and Theo and Mum living with Nan because they said it was better for school even though

Nan's house is a twenty-minute drive across town and Dad's flat is a ten-minute walk from the school gates.

But the flat Dad chose only has one bedroom. The silence that follows says more than my words.

Amy turns to cut across the same park Bazza and I did earlier. "I know what's happening is hard," she says – no trace of sarcasm in her voice, "but trust me: two happy halves are better than one miserable whole."

Her gentle words soothe the raw edges where resentment's been sawing away at me. It's the first time anyone's talked to me about this without getting awkward and changing the subject or trying to cheer me up – or doing so much of the talking that I never get to say anything.

"Thanks," I say, following her round the cycle barrier and out on to the street.

"Any time." And I hope she means it – I've had conversations before where the person's gone back to ignoring me once we're in uniform.

We've nearly reached my old house and I wonder about telling Amy that this is where I used to live, before I moved in with my nan…

Until she stops. Right on the drive.

"So," she says, tucking the strands of hair that have blown loose behind one ear. "This is me."

*

The first thing I notice is that the door's shut on the coat cupboard when it should be stuffed to bursting with boots and jackets and ski-wear we never bothered putting away between holidays.

"Kitchen's this way." Amy nods down the hall.

I know, I want to say. I should have got the words out on the drive, but she asked me if I'd like to warm up and I panicked she'd take it back if she found out this was where I'd lived – and I wanted to come inside *so* badly...

"Sam?" Amy turns to see I'm still stranded on the doormat.

"I – er – shouldn't I take my shoes off?"

"Don't worry about it – we're recarpeting."

Recarpeting? All of a sudden I'm absurdly offended on behalf of something I never gave a second thought to. Taking my shoes off in protest, I pad through to the kitchen where marble surfaces glitter under the expensive spots Dad insisted on. There's whining and scratching coming from the door that leads into the big back lobby and I stop in the middle of the floor to say, somewhat stupidly, "You've got a dog?"

"Are you allergic?" Amy pauses. The whining escalates to frenzied barks and I shake my head. "Good."

As the door opens, a muscular bullet shoots through the gap, spiralling round Amy before running over to me, snuffling, barking and half jumping up at me, completely disregarding Amy's, "Violet, *no*. Down. *No*."

An odd name for an English bull terrier.

"She won't bite." Amy crouches down and fusses the dog, still talking to me. "She doesn't like being shut in, but she can't be left in the kitchen until we put a child gate up by the lounge or she'd trash the joint. Wouldn't you, Violet?"

Violet pants happily as Amy scrubs her knuckles on the dog's snout.

"Right." She stands to open the fridge. "What can I get you? Greg's got some craft ale if you want?"

The face she's pulling doesn't make it sound appealing.

"Tea's fine – I'm not drinking tonight anyway." I raise my arm and ping my rubber medical band. "Type 1 diabetes."

"Bummer."

I shrug. It is what it is – it's not like I *couldn't* drink if I was careful, I just prefer not to. I've had hypos ruin enough parties as a kid for me not to risk it now I'm older.

Amy goes round opening cupboards and looking for mugs, joking about not knowing where anything is, the dog trotting after her while I stand there like a muppet. She finds the mugs in the same cupboard we used, which spins me out. It's getting weirder by the second that I haven't told her I used to live here…

But as Amy walks over, Violet darts under her feet, so that Amy has to stumble to catch herself, tea sloshing out of the mugs.

"Violet!" Amy tuts at where the tea's soaking into her top. "Can you keep an eye on the dog while I go and sort this out? The top's Mum's and she'll kill me if I've stained it."

*

I hear the taps go on upstairs and I exchange a glance with Violet, who immediately trots off down the corridor towards the lounge. Two seconds and I'm off after her…

But what I see stops me as effectively as a child gate would have stopped the dog.

The lounge stretches from French windows at the back to a massive bay window at the front and I'd been expecting to see an echo of how it used to be, but this set-up is so far from familiar I could be in a different house entirely.

Why would they put the sofa there? Or the TV? And there's a dining table at one end, even though there's a whole room for that on the other side of the kitchen. There's books on the shelves instead of ornaments, mirrors instead of pictures and…

Where's the tree?

There are no cards or decorations – not even a tasteful nativity scene that my nan would approve of – and the sight of it swoops through me, as bleak and melancholy as a midwinter carol.

"Sam?" Amy's voice makes me jump. There was a time when no one could possibly have snuck up on me in this house. When she sees Violet looking guilty on the sofa, Amy snaps her fingers and the dog scuttles shame-tailed back to the kitchen.

"Sorry," I say. "I tried to stop her." And then, "Where's your tree? Or ... are you, like, not into the birth of Jesus?"

Amy laughs. She's changed into a big jumper that's sliding off one shoulder, the cuffs curled round her fingers. "Totally into it, but Mum's old-school. Nothing up until Christmas Eve."

"Not even cards?" Although the answer is all around, on the empty mantelpiece and windowsills.

Amy waves a hand at a sprawl of envelopes in the middle of the dining-room table. "Waiting to be opened on the twenty-fourth. Mum insists it's tradition to leave it until the last minute, but she's like that whatever the time of year."

As we head back to the kitchen, I ask where her mum and Greg are.

"Some Christmas ball back home – or where home used to be. In Edinburgh." Amy sips what's left of her drink before registering my confusion. "Someone needs to dog-sit."

"And they were fine leaving you on your own?" I can't imagine either of my parents being so cool about it – even less so my nan. It was hard enough persuading her to let me stay over at Bazza's.

Amy nods. "It's not like I'm going to have a party, is it? I don't know anyone."

"You do now." I raise my mug in a 'cheers' kind of gesture.

"Do I? All I know is that you don't like your nan keeping bread in the fridge."

"It's a very important detail." But the chill I'm going for is ruffled by the way the tops of her cheeks crinkle when she smiles. I gulp my tea carelessly and cough. "So – er – what do you want to know about me?"

"Anything – what you like to do for fun, what's your favourite film or food or animal. What superpower you'd choose. Where you grew up…"

"Here." I say it before I chicken out.

"OK, that was a bad question…" She hasn't understood.

"I meant *here*." I point down at the floor. "In this house."

She thinks I'm joking. You would, wouldn't you?

But then she gets that I'm not.

"Why didn't you say?" Amy stares at me like there are more secrets to see.

"Seemed a bit rude to bring it up ... like, 'Oh, come for a drink in my house,' and I'm all like, 'Actually, that used to be *my* house,' and –" I'm floundering – "it seemed weird."

She doesn't say anything and whatever groove we'd found is lost as I turn my mug round, imagining the handle ticking off seconds on the face of a clock. When a minute has passed, I say, "Bazza might wonder where I've got to…"

Like he's even noticed I've gone.

"Maybe you should head back, then," Amy says without looking up.

"Um – can I use the loo before I go?" I sound like a little kid.

"You know where it is." And I can feel her gaze following me out to the back lobby. Stepping over Violet's bedding and into the cloakroom, I find everything the same as ever, right down to the brand of liquid soap. Closing my eyes, I rest my weight on the sink. I wish I hadn't come inside, spoiling my memories of the past with looking at the present, comparing lives as if there's a choice between one and the other. This isn't my home any more and all I'm doing is cocking everything up.

Amy's standing in the doorway to the kitchen when I come out.

"Are you going back to the party because you want to, or because of me?"

"Um…" I say, because I'm that articulate.

"I mean, you *can*, but don't leave because you think I've got the hump about the house. It's not a big deal." She narrows her eyes. "Unless you stalked me at the party just for this?"

"You were the one who spoke to me!"

"A good stalker would have orchestrated that." Her head's tilted, lips twisting prettily to the side as she suppresses a smile.

"I'm not a good stalker," I say, grinning as I add, "I'm deeply mediocre."

I get a laugh for that and when Amy tucks her hair behind her ear, I see she's pinked up a little, even though it's cooler out here, surrounded by windows and tiles.

"Well, if Bazza's not going to miss you too much,

would you like to hang out a bit longer?" She sounds careless, but I think of her going to Bazza's party because it was better being alone in a crowded room than being alone in an empty house.

Maybe having my nan around isn't as bad as the alternative.

I message Bazza to let him know where I am as Amy makes more tea, talking all the while about her old house – tall and narrow with more staircases than floorspace. I like the burr of her voice, the way she smiles or laughs at the things she says, and I could sit here, feet resting under the hot bulk of a bull terrier, and listen to her all night long. When her words slow to silence and she looks at me across the table, her eyes sparkle and I notice the way one of her teeth crooks over the other.

"So, do you want to have a nosey, then?" Amy nods to the door.

*

Amy says the dining room will be her mum's office because Greg's already snagged the other one. She means the den.

It's upsetting to see a room designed for pleasure put to use as an office: the flatscreen replaced by a world map with coloured threads pinned across the oceans; a printer and paper shredder, and piles of files and folders where there should be a sofa and beanbags. Greg's desk takes up so much space that it's hard to imagine a pool table ever fitting in here.

But if you look closely enough, if you know what you're looking for, you can still see the faint spatter on one wall where Theo opened a can of Coke I'd shaken up, and the burnt spot on the carpet where I dropped a match.

"I spent a lot of time in here," I tell Amy.

Upstairs, the dog – who Amy's become lax about disciplining – potters into the master bedroom and wuffles around the carpet, but I'm drawn towards a different door, one pin-pocked and blotchy from Blu-Tack.

"This was my brother's room." I scan the walls, remembering pictures that aren't there.

"It's going to be my sister's," Amy says.

"Where's all her stuff?" The only thing in here is a futon.

"With her, at uni. She's putting off coming back to a house she doesn't feel is hers." There's a lot of feeling behind that sentence.

"It'll feel like yours soon," I say.

"Will it?" Amy looks so sad that I push myself harder to find something that will help.

"It'll feel like yours once you discover its secrets, when you come home and know by the shape of the silence whether there's anyone else here, when you stain the carpet or mark the wall. It'll feel like your home when your sister's back and you're putting up old decorations somewhere new, building a bridge between the Christmases you used to have and the one you're having now…"

It's the most I've said since I set foot inside and I trail off because somewhere along the line I stopped talking about Amy's new home and started talking about mine – Nan's. A home where the owner let us put up a tree too big for the front room so we'd have enough branches for all our old ornaments. A home where our cards are crammed on to shelves we don't own as if they're as important as the ones addressed to Nan.

Amy looks at me and I heat up under her scrutiny.

"Could you introduce me to the house?" she says with a smile. "I'd like to get to know it better."

I start with the creaky spot on the landing, moving on to the step you can trust on your way down, but not on your way up. In the bathroom I show her the secret ledge behind the boiler and the knack to flushing the toilet. Then we get to my room – Amy's room – where tonight's full moon casts shadowed gridlines on the carpet. Before Amy can reach for the light, I guide her to the spot by the window.

"Feel that?"

"Yes," she says, and I become hyper aware of the soft material of her jumper on my skin, the cold moonlight bleaching us into black and white.

"The hot water pipes run under here."

"Violet'll like that." Amy shifts to look through the faux-leaded glass to the back garden below, asking me what the neighbours are like.

"That side's an old couple who are well into gardening – I used to help them out, cutting the grass, lifting things, weeding and whatever. Washed their car, too."

"That was nice of you."

"Not that nice – I got paid. I was saving up for a

watch." I pull back the sleeve of my top to show her. The face is scratched and the strap needs replacing, but this watch was the first thing that truly belonged to me. The first thing I *earned* without Dad swooping in and making up the difference.

"My dad wants to buy me a new one for Christmas," I say.

"I like this one," Amy says quietly.

And I nod, because I do, too. There was a time when I measured how valuable stuff was by how much it cost, but when they got divorced – when we had the chat about money and how we didn't really have any – it made me think about all those things Dad had spunked money on … sports equipment and TVs and computers and pool tables. Things worth nothing when you can't afford a home to put them in.

Amy frowns at my watch. "Is that the real time?"

"No, I like to sync with a different time zone to the one I'm in." I'm getting better at this flirting business.

She slaps me lightly on the arm. "Violet needs to go out."

*

The cold has more weight to it than before, pressing through the material of my jacket. I stand with Amy at the top of the back steps, watching the ghost-white blur of the dog, zigzagging around the lawn.

In my mind, though, I'm the one who's on the lawn. I'm mastering a Pelé flick and learning to control the ball with my chest. I'm a child with a pump-action water pistol, fighting with my friends. I'm a dutiful son carrying a tray of iced drinks to where my parents laze in the dappled shade of the trees that line the back fence. I'm a big brother, yelling at Theo to come in for tea. I'm a teenager, standing here with a girl and wondering what it would be like to kiss her.

"Violet!" Amy calls out. "Where are you going...?"

She puts one hand to her mouth and lets out a short, painfully sharp whistle that the dog ignores, her solid behind wagging away as she dives through a bush.

Amy groans, but I'm grinning.

"Come on!" I run across the lawn, holding out my hand for Amy to join me. "There's one more secret to show you..."

There's the gentle slap of feet on the grass, then her hand, hot from her pocket, slides into mine and I'm pushing back familiar branches, bare and scratchy, to show Amy the gap running between the bushes and the fence.

"This used to be our special tunnel," I half whisper, thinking of the few summers where Theo's idea of fun overlapped mine and we would come back here to hide from our parents.

The dog's up ahead and I tug Amy with me, glancing back to see her smiling wide and bright in the dark, a dry leaf caught in her hair.

"I'd have loved this place as a kid," she says. Then she squeezes my hand and adds, "Kind of love it now."

At the end of the fenceline I let go to push aside more branches, stamping across the back of the compost heap, following Violet as if she's the one who knows where we're going. Amy and I are squashed over and panting, breath as loud as the rustle of the bushes and the crack of twigs beneath our feet. We reach the far corner of the garden – inaccessible by any other route – and emerge into the space beneath the tree that stands there.

Amy squints at the sky through the web of branches as she walks towards the trunk and runs her palm over a series of thick lines scored into the bark.

"Is this where you measured yourselves?"

"It was Theo's idea."

Mum had painted over the doorframe where she'd been measuring us and he'd wanted somewhere more permanent. Somewhere our history would live on no matter how many coats of paint went up. Somewhere that belonged to us ... and now belongs to someone else.

I look at Amy for a long moment, appreciating how she's quietly allowed me to relive the ghosts of Christmases – and springs and summers and autumns – past. It's something I'd like to repay.

"Let's measure you," I say.

It's not exactly accurate, using the flat of my hand as a measure and gouging a line with the keys from my pocket, but that's not what matters.

"You're almost as tall as me," I say, not looking at the tree, too distracted by the girl, taking in the strong line of her eyebrows that, even now, have a slightly sarcastic slant to them, her eyes curving up in the corners like she's teasing me with just a look.

I've never wanted to kiss a girl as much as I want to

kiss Amy Sparrow and I let that feeling push me closer until her breath becomes mine and our lips meet, her hands on my jumper pulling me in…

And her dog barking and scrabbling up my leg.

We part, shy and breathless and smiling, and we leave our tree – our kiss – and push back through the secret tunnel until the three of us are out in the open air once more. Amy points to the snow spots in the sky, drifting down, light as ash on the air.

"Amy," I say, my heart stuttering at the way she turns to look at me. I reach into my pocket and pull out my keys, unwinding one from its split ring and holding it up. The key to the front door that I cut for myself – the one I kept secret because I wanted to keep the house.

I place the key in her palm and fold her fingers over. "It's all yours."

*

Hours later, my throat sore from talking all night, my body fizzing from lack of sleep and the memory of what it was like to kiss Amy under the tree, on the lawn and in the kitchen, on the sofa and the front step, I turn down Nan's road and speed up to a half-jog.

I let Bazza know I'd pick my stuff up later, but I sneak into Nan's house, wanting to surprise them.

They're up already – Theo's an irritatingly early riser – and the chat and laughter coming from the kitchen disguises the sound of me kicking off my shoes and dropping my jacket on the stairs. I follow the hiss of a frying pan and the smell of toast until I'm in the door to see Mum and Theo at the table, poring over whatever game's on the back of the cereal packet, Nan with her back to me by the toaster.

"Who's for toast?" she calls out.

"I am," I say, enjoying the way Theo cackles as Mum nearly jumps out of her skin and Nan turns round to eyeball me.

"Thought your father was to pick you up from your friend's house, Samuel," she says. I hear the veneer of irritation with which she varnishes her words, but now, when I listen – when I *look* – I understand that Nan's feelings are built on something much more solid than that.

"Felt like coming home, didn't I?" I say.

If Only in My Dreams

*

Marcus Sedgwick

It was the black.

It was other things, too. It was the way the sun rose and set fifteen times a day. It was the near absence of taste. It was the claustrophobia of living in a confined metal tube, the intensity of sharing that tube with two others for months on end. It was the long, long silences, cut up by bursts from the radio. It was all of these things and more, but above all else, it was the black that was to blame.

It was there all the time, and yesterday, when Grey had made the EVA, it only got worse – the black at his back. Floating on his tether, as he made his way down the length of the station, he'd seen Amira give him a brief thumbs up through the Destiny window, before she returned to Commander Hirsch's side to monitor the spacewalk.

– You know this is only the third EVA on Christmas Eve, Grey? I mean, ever.

So much Commander Hirsch had told him as they'd prepped the suit. It didn't make him any happier about the fact he had to go outside the station, work his way to the end of the P5/6 truss and try to fix the fault with the solar array there, the blackness pawing at his back the whole time.

It took five hours, during which the sun rose and set, rose and set, rose and set three times in all as they flew round the dark side of the Earth, each time emerging to a new and uncaring sun, clipping its way up out of the planet, each time filling Grey with the sense that they had been doing just this for several billions of years. And each time, he'd been caught night-dreaming, as Hirsch had been asking something about the EVA.

– Grey, you still out there, buddy?

– Yeah. I'm here. Go again.

– We need the reading on the array.

– Uh, yeah. Copy that. Give me a minute…

– OK. Copy. As long as you're still out there.

Am I still here, Grey thought, am I? Yes, I am. I am. I know I am because I can hear myself thinking, and that means I'm here.

But as he took the reading of the array's angle and as he found that it wasn't moving freely due to debris in the joint, which had happened before, and as he cleaned it and lubricated it so it would turn to the sun as it was supposed to, he didn't feel anywhere at all. All the time, the black kept pawing and clawing at his back, even through his suit, even through Hirsch talking to him, even as he made his way back into the airlock, array fixed and working well. As he divested himself, with Amira's help, of the suit, he knew he'd brought a bit more black back inside the station with him.

He said nothing of this to Amira, of course, nor to Commander Hirsch.

– You OK, Grey? Amira had asked him when they took his helmet off.

– Yeah, sure. Just tired.

– Well, your shift's done. Get some rest.

He'd nodded and smiled at Amira and then left her to finish stowing the EVA suit while he drifted to his pod. On his way there, he'd stopped by the largest window in the station, the Cupola window, and bathed his eyes with Earth until Hirsch told him to get to his bunk and get some sleep.

– Just stopped to say goodnight, he said. I was on my way there.

Except… Except it was only when he started tying himself into his sleeping rack did he realize that the Cupola wasn't on the way from the airlock to his pod. And he also realized that Commander Hirsch hadn't pointed that out.

He knew why that was. There were just the three of them. The days of crews of six had gone; expense was being trimmed wherever possible, and that included running the station half full. That put extra work into their hands, of course, and that was OK, because there's only so much you can do with your spare time in a space station anyway: exercise more, read more, email more, phone home more, and there's something weird about an astronaut who calls home more than home calls him. But there was extra pressure on the three of them, and Hirsch was a good commander; it didn't work to fly by the book on every little thing. Three people, alone in a metal tube, flying round the Earth at 17,000 miles an hour for six months; you had to allow some slack, here and there.

Grey told himself to be more careful, though. He had always had the sense of not being like other astronauts. He was British, for one thing, and that was still a rarity, but then Amira was Pakistani, and a woman, too, so she pretty much trumped him for rarity. It wasn't where they were from that counted, he knew, or the fact that his was his first mission, because the same was true of Amira. It was something else; it was the way that Amira and Hirsch were so professional, so focused, and yes, he was a trained pilot and an able scientist, too, but somehow he'd never got over the wonders of space travel. It still delighted him to glide through the station, weightless. And he still amused himself when no one was watching by squirting a bubble of water out from his drinking tube, letting it quiver in the air in front of him like a living silvery thing, until he gobbled it up. And he could never not look at Earth. He would stop at Destiny or Cupola whenever he could and grab even a single second of the view. His sleep pod had no window, unlike the disused Russian ones on the other side of the station, which each had a view; some of Earth, yes, but some of…

Maybe it was better not to have a window. He would either spend all the time he should be sleeping staring at the blue-green ball where seven billion people lived, or he'd be able to see the blackness, all the time, and it would be able to see him.

So he was careful not to mention these kinds of things to Hirsch and Amira, because he did not want them thinking he was strange, he did not want them worrying about him, because there were only the three of them, and they all needed to know that everything was fine, just fine.

It was for these reasons that Grey did not talk about his dream that night, the night after the EVA when he had brought some more of the black back inside the station with him. But because he did not voice his dream, it stayed all the more strongly with him, unable to be let out. It vibrated inside him all morning, as he did his morning exercises, and ate his breakfast with the others, in silence, during which he was lost in his thoughts of it, right up until the point at which Hirsch said, "Happy Christmas".

Grey blinked.

– I thought... he said. Then, I mean, you're Jewish.

– Doesn't mean I can't wish you a happy Christmas, does it?

Grey smiled.

– No, I guess not.

– Going to be a quiet one for you this year.

Grey nodded.

– An English atheist, an American Jew and a Pakistani Muslim, he said. It sounds like the beginning of a racist joke.

Amira laughed.

– What's the punchline? she asked.

Grey shrugged.

– I'm not sure I'd want to know.

Hirsch cleared his throat, melodramatically.

– 'Twas the night before Christmas, he announced. When all through the house—

– Commander, what are you doing? asked Amira.

– It's called poetry, and I am reciting it for the benefit of Grey here, in order to give him some old-timey Christmas-type feelings. Instead of a present, because I don't have a present.

– Oh, said Amira. I see.

– When all through the house, not a creature was

stirring, not even a mouse. The stockings were hung by the chimney with—

– Commander? asked Grey.

Hirsch pretended to be annoyed.

– Now what?

– Nothing, Commander. Only… Why do you know that poem?

– Because we all had to learn to recite it in third grade. Yes, even us Jews. Can I go on now?

– Oh, yeah. Sure. Thanks.

And so Hirsch did. He recited 'A Visit from St Nicholas', all fifty-something lines of it, and as he did, Amira's smile grew wider and Grey's gaze drifted until, when he finished, they both cheered and applauded as if they were crazy, then all three of them got the giggles while the station flew on at 17,000 miles an hour, and the sun came up for the second time that day and the black yawned away to infinity, infinity, infinity.

When they finished laughing, Amira clapped her hands together twice, so sharply that Grey and Hirsch snapped to attention.

– Now I want to give you a present, too, she said.

– Don't tell me you learned to sing 'White Christmas'

when you were six, said Grey, or I might die laughing.

Amira stuck out her tongue at him.

– I did not. Sadly. However, I will tell you a folk tale from where I was born and that will be my present to you. It's about snow.

– Snow? asked Grey.

– Yes, there's snow in Pakistan, too. Not just in your Christmas songs.

And she told them a tale, a very old one, about a king of the place known as Gilgit. It was a strange story about Azru, the youngest of three fairy brothers, who becomes human and destroys an evil tyrant by using fire to melt the snow wherein his soul is contained. In doing so, he abolishes the rites of human sacrifice the tyrant had insisted upon and frees the tyrant's daughter. They fall in love, and Grey saw that it was the sort of story that finishes with a happy ending.

– Thank you, he said, very seriously. That was very beautiful.

– It's a little strange, Amira said. But it's the only story I know with snow in it. And you have snow at Christmas, don't you, in England?

Grey smiled, but it was not a happy smile.

– We used to, he said. When I was a boy. But they decided to do away with it.

– Who did? asked Amira, not understanding.

– I don't know, said Grey. Whoever decides these things. Whoever it was who screwed our climate up.

– Oh, said Amira, I see. Then Grey felt bad, because he believed that with that touch of bitterness he'd tainted the presents he'd been given. So he decided he ought to give something back.

– I'd like to tell you a story, too, he said.

– It's your Christmas, said Hirsch. Definitely not mine.

– Yes, but Christmas is about giving presents. Not receiving them.

– Isn't that the same thing? asked Amira.

– Depends on your point of view, I suppose, said Hirsch. OK, then, give us a present. Tell us a story.

Grey looked at them both, hesitating as the black rushed around inside him, forever, and all he could think of was his dream; that dream, that terrible dream he'd had the night before, from which he'd woken, but would never really wake from. Not ever.

– What is it? asked Hirsch.

Grey didn't want to say, he didn't want to say anything. It was just the three of them in their little floating tube and it wouldn't do to get weird, or say something strange, and his dream was right up there. And he even knew why he'd had it, he really thought he knew why, but that didn't make it any less powerful. He knew all the stories about astronauts, of course, right back to some of the guys from the golden days – the Apollo missions – and how there was something about floating in space and looking down on the Earth that could unnerve the sanest of them. It was something about seeing the planet – with everyone and everything it had ever been – adrift on the black ocean of the universe. Some had turned to God, but Grey knew that route wasn't open for him – he had too much imagination for that. But what was there instead? There was nothing. There was just the infinite black nothing arcing away into endlessness behind his back as he peered down through the Destiny 20-inch window.

– You OK? Hirsch said.

– Yeah, said Grey, I'm really fine. It's just... I mean, I had this dream last night and...

He fell into silence, which lasted until Hirsch said:

– I know what you mean. I have some real strange ones when I'm up here.

– You do? asked Grey.

Hirsch nodded.

– This is my third expedition and there've always been dreams. But I gotta tell you, nothing beats the one I had last night.

He slapped Grey on the shoulder, gently, left his hand there for a moment and it was weird, very weird to know that both men were realizing that they hadn't touched any other human being for six months.

– Tell us your dream, said Grey.

Hirsch told his dream, his nightmare vision of the Earth.

– I was asleep, he began. In my dream, I was asleep, right here on the station and then something woke me up. I don't know what it was, but I felt like I heard someone scream and I woke up. And I went to Cupola to look out of the big window, and there was the Earth.

Already Grey was looking at the commander with growing unease, but he could only listen in silent and mounting horror as Hirsch went on.

– And the Earth was sitting there, looking just like

it always does, the sun was on its face and it was green and the oceans were blue, just like normal and then it started... Well... I mean, it started to rot.

– What? whispered Grey. It started to...

Hirsch threw up his hands.

– I'm no writer, he said. I mean, it just started to rot. Bits were turning black and kind of shrivelling, and—

– Collapsing, said Grey, interrupting.

– Yeah, said Hirsch, but how did you—

Grey ignored him, he ignored the question, but he finished the dream for him.

– It turned black, he said. First the land, and you could see mountains collapsing, and then when they collapsed, the oceans started to turn black. The blackness seeped into the oceans like they were stagnating and thickening and then finally the whole Earth started to tremble and shake, somehow, and then it imploded. It just imploded, sucked into itself, and all that was left behind was a quivering hole in space.

Hirsch stared at him, and there was a much longer silence then, until finally the commander asked a question he already knew the answer to.

– How did you know that?

– Because it was my dream, too, Grey said. Exactly.

The two men stared at each other for a very long time, and so unnerved were they that it took them a very long time to notice that Amira was holding her hand to her mouth, tears running down her face.

– What? asked Grey. What's wrong?

It was very hard to hear Amira's reply, because she spoke so softly, but when she repeated herself, they just made out what she was saying.

– I dreamt it, too, she whispered. I dreamt it, too.

Grey realized that Hirsch still had his hand on his shoulder. He turned and reached a hand towards Amira and then, in all silence, the three of them held hands in a ring, and the station flew on at 17,000 miles an hour around the place we all called home, and the blackness hammered itself around them, infinite, infinite, infinite.

Family You Choose

*

Cat Clarke

Starter
Paneer bhajis, mixed vegetable pakoras,
cheese and pineapple on sticks

"Could you pass the ketchup, Effie?"

Who the hell has ketchup on a bhaji? I reach for the bottle, knocking my elbow against my glass. Red wine spills all over my plate and starts spreading across the table with alarming speed.

"Oh God, I'm so sorry!"

"It's fine!" Sarah is up from her chair and at my side in the blink of an eye. She swipes her paper napkin over the table. Some drops hit the wooden floor, but the dog, Rocky, makes swift work of them.

My cheeks feel like they're on fire, and they were already flushed after half a glass of wine. Still a total lightweight.

I dab at a few spots of wine with my napkin, but Sarah tells me not to bother. "It adds character. Anyway, this table has been a write-off ever since the Great Pan Incident of 2013… *Hasn't* it, Priya?" Priya just smiles and shrugs. It's obvious that the big black mark in the middle of the table was her fault. When I look closer, I see all kinds of dents and scratches in the dark brown wood. It's a table with history, that's for sure. Unlike the glass and steel monstrosity my parents bought last month.

The guy sitting opposite me smiles the tiniest smile you can imagine, then quickly covers his mouth as if embarrassed about it. His name is Lionel and he is the neatest, tidiest-looking person you've ever seen. He also hasn't said a single word since he got here. AJ introduced us, and Lionel smiled and nodded and gave a little wave, but that was it. He came in carrying a cardboard box oh-so-carefully, like there was an unexploded bomb inside. Everyone seemed very excited about it, so I'm guessing it's not a bomb after all. I'm hoping for tiny adorable kittens.

"Here you go, Effie," says Sarah, putting a new plate in front of me and piling it with more food than I could ever possibly eat. "Red-wine infused bhajis sounds like one of AJ's creations, but maybe that little experiment is best saved for another day."

AJ is too busy stuffing a ketchup-slathered bhaji in his mouth to respond. I smile politely and wonder if coming here was a mistake.

The Annual Waifs and Strays Anti-Christmas Dinner. That's what AJ said when he invited me. "At least, that's what *I* call it, anyway." He rolled his eyes like he thought it was stupid, which made me wonder why he would invite me to something he thought was stupid. He didn't seem surprised when I said I already had plans on the Saturday before Christmas. He also didn't seem surprised when I messaged him an hour ago to ask if it would be OK if I turned up after all. AJ seems like a pretty laidback sort of guy. He's certainly laidback enough about the history assignment we're working on together.

Lionel isn't eating bhajis and samosas like the rest of us. On his plate there's what looks to be some sort of foil hedgehog, with the spikes made out of cocktail sticks. Each cocktail stick skewers a segment of pineapple and a cube of bright orange cheese.

He offers the platter around (silently, of course) and I take one, just to be polite.

AJ's mums, Sarah and Priya, have been nothing but welcoming. They keep checking I'm OK, and that I don't mind Rocky drooling on my Converse. I watch them joke and laugh with AJ and it hurts my heart a little. Things used to be like that with my parents. At least, I think they did.

Priya takes the piss out of AJ's new haircut and AJ insists she's just jealous of his 'fresh trim'. He looks to me for back-up and I say that I quite like it.

The 'quite' sets Priya off laughing again for some reason.

Marjorie tuts. "Leave the poor boy alone, Priya! I think his ... um ... trim looks very fresh indeed."

After the hilarity has died down a bit, Marjorie turns to me. "So what's your story, Miss Effie?" Marjorie is seventy-six years old, a fact she's mentioned at least five times since we sat down. She used to be a doctor, which she's only mentioned once. She makes me nervous – old people sometimes do.

"My what?"

"Your story. What makes you *you*? Regale us with

fascinating tales of adventure and mischief. Or debauchery. I wouldn't mind a bit of that. The only debauchery I get these days is watching Jeremy Kyle."

My phone rings in my pocket.

"Saved by the bell!" Marjorie laughs.

My first thought is: Fran. But of course it's not Fran, because it's the wrong ring tone. And because she hates me now. At least, I assume she does.

It's my mother. I hit the button to end the call and put the phone on silent.

Someone's filled up my glass without me even noticing. I take a gulp of wine and turn to Marjorie. "I don't have a story."

"Everyone has a story, dear."

Hmm. Girl Meets Girl. Girl comes out to parents who act totally cool about it, but are actually anything but. Parents are painfully uncomfortable and embarrassed whenever said Girlfriend is around. Girl eventually breaks up with Girlfriend out of sheer stupidity, parents act like douchebags, as if no real feelings could have possibly been involved in the relationship. Girl walks out of house an hour before eighteenth birthday party arranged by said douchebag parents for family who happen to be completely unaware of girl's queerness. Girl goes to have dinner with a bunch of strangers instead.

I don't think that's quite the kind of story Marjorie is after.

*

Main course
Black bean tacos, AJ's guacamole of wonder,
pickled red onions and assorted bits and bobs

I was expecting some kind of curry after that starter, but the weirdness continues. Rocky is at my feet, scarfing down a taco stuffed with dog food and cheese, and everyone is acting like this is a perfectly normal thing for a dog to eat.

AJ's guacamole *is* indeed a thing of wonder. All of the food is really good, actually. Much better than what I'd be getting at home. Mum went totally overboard – as usual. I'd have been happy with some sausage rolls and tortilla chips. Or proper food like this, made by someone who cares. I told her I didn't want fancy canapés or whatever, but she wouldn't listen. She was adamant that she wanted to get a caterer in – probably to impress her snobby sisters. She didn't care what I wanted to eat at the party, or who I wanted to invite.

Mum's not going to forgive me for this in a hurry. Showing her up in front of her sisters. She's only got herself to blame though – insisting on going ahead with the party when I'd said I couldn't face it. I check the time on the tinsel-decked clock above the kitchen door: 6.07 p.m. The party officially starts in twenty-three minutes, although knowing my family, I bet people are already there.

Lionel is tucking in with gusto, piling up his tacos with toppings. I want to tell him that I like his bowtie, but I don't want to embarrass him. He still hasn't said a word, but he looks perfectly content. Everyone else talks – a lot. So far topics have included: coriander and whether it is in fact the food of the devil (Sarah is not a fan, the rest of us love it); UKIP (no one is a fan, *obviously*); Marjorie's son Harry who wants her to go and live in a care home (only marginally more popular than UKIP, except with Marjorie who says, "I do love him, though," somewhat halfheartedly); tattoos.

Priya has a full sleeve on each arm. The tattoos are

incredible, but I suppose you'd expect nothing less on a tattoo artist. I ask her if it's scary, trusting her skin to someone else.

"Nah, I like having other people's art on me."

"I'd like to get a tattoo," I say. I've never even thought about it before, but suddenly, two glasses of wine down, it seems like the best idea in the world. "Would you do it for me?"

Sarah puts her hand on top of Priya's and says, "You'd have to join the waiting list. What is it now? Six months? Seven?"

"Wow, you must be *really* good."

"She is," says Sarah, and you can tell she's so proud of Priya. I think about how proud I felt watching Fran up onstage and I wonder if it's the same thing. Or is it different, what they've got? Is it deeper, truer, *more*?

They make an odd-looking couple, Sarah and Priya. Sarah looks like a proper grown-up and has some serious job that apparently involves a lot of spreadsheets. Priya looks like a total badass. Tattoos, piercings and eyeliner skills that I can only dream of. I know opposites are meant to attract, but it never seems to be that way at school. The couples I know tend to look like matching sets. Even Fran and me.

I didn't even know AJ had two mums. He kept that little nugget of information to himself. Maybe he's trying to make a point, like, "This is the future you *could* have had, if you hadn't chosen to dump your perfect girlfriend."

"I've got a tattoo, you know," says Marjorie with a sly smile.

Even Priya looks shocked. They proceed to guess what – and where – it is. The only ones who say nothing are Lionel and me. He meets my eye and smiles, and there's something about the kindness there that makes me want to cry.

It's on her boob. The tattoo is on her boob. Nobody guessed that. Probably because thinking about the boobs of a seventy-six-year-old woman seems a bit disrespectful. She had it done on her seventieth birthday. It's a chaffinch.

"Ron used to call me his little bird. I wanted to... Well, I suppose I just wanted to remember. What it was like to belong with someone. What it was like to be loved."

Suddenly the atmosphere is all melancholy, and I really do want to cry. I think I could cry among these people and they wouldn't even blink. They wouldn't tell me to plaster a smile on my face and pretend. They would let me be sad, because sometimes it's OK to be sad. That's what Mum doesn't understand.

"We love you, Marj," says Sarah. "You know that."

"I know, dear. And I love you."

Then Lionel does something and I can't decide if it's the oddest thing he's done since he got here, or the coolest. He puts his thumbs and forefingers together to make a heart sign. And Marjorie smiles and does exactly the same thing.

"All right, all right, enough of this feelings malarkey," says Priya, earning a high five from AJ. "Effie, are you sure you've had enough to eat? There's plenty more if you want it. And make sure you take some leftovers home with you. It always tastes better the next day anyway."

"Then why didn't you make it yesterday?" Sarah laughs.

"Smartarse."

Suddenly Sarah slaps her own forehead with such force it makes me wince. "Oh my God, we forgot about the toast!"

AJ rolls his eyes. "It's OK, Mum. I don't think the world is going to end if you don't make your little speech."

"It's tradition!"

"You hate tradition!"

"I make an exception for this one." Sarah sticks her tongue out at her son. "But I'll keep it short."

"Thank God for that," AJ murmurs, but he's smiling.

"So this is what, the fifth time we've hosted this little gathering? I know that this time of year can be tough for various reasons – for each and every one of us. But this always turns out to be one of the highlights of *my* year, and I'm so happy to be able to share it with you. There may be a couple of people missing today, but I'm delighted to welcome Effie into the fold—"

"Sounds a bit like a cult, doesn't it?" Priya quips, topping up everyone's glasses.

"Anywaaaaay, as I was saying before I was so rudely interrupted… I'd like to make a toast. To friends – the family you choose."

Everyone raises their glass and clinks them together in the middle of the table. "To friends!" we all echo. Except Lionel.

I take another swig of my wine and decide that this will be my last glass. It's going to my head, softening me into a marshmallow-mushy idiot who's happy to be here and grateful to these strangers for treating me better than my own family.

The front door slams open and someone stumbles in. It takes me a second or two to recognize him. Like when you see your English teacher at the cinema. There's no way Serge Black belongs here. Onstage in some sweaty club, guitar slung low, singing my favourite song? Yes. Crouched on the floor in AJ's living room, being slobbered on by Rocky the dog? No.

But he *is* here. Wearing a hoodie, tracksuit bottoms and questionable trainers – the sort of clothes you'd never see him wearing onstage. I should know – I've seen him play four times in the past year. Well, three and a half. Fran and I missed a fair bit of the last gig. (Her fault, not mine.)

Maybe the clothes are some kind of disguise? Seems a bit excessive – he's not exactly famous. Not yet anyway. He's teetering on the edge of fame. Word has it that several major labels want to sign him, but he's biding his time, weighing up his options.

"Rocky, mate, we made a deal! Kisses are fine, but I draw the line at your tongue entering my mouth, OK?"

AJ sees me gawping and laughs. "Told you you'd want to come."

Part of me wishes Fran were here to see this. But AJ probably wouldn't have invited me if he hadn't found me crying in the American History section of the library, and I wouldn't have been crying in the American History section of the library if I wasn't already regretting breaking up with Fran. Fran couldn't possibly be here, so I should just stop thinking about her. I can try, anyway.

Serge kisses Priya, Sarah and Marjorie on the cheeks, nods at Lionel and grabs AJ in some sort of headlock that I think is meant to be affectionate. AJ shuffles along on the bench to make space.

"Did I miss the toast? Shit, I *love* the toast." He reaches across the table and grabs Priya's glass and holds it up. "To friends! Friends who are there for you when your family – and your entire life, in fact – is an utter shitshow. Cheers, big ears!" He downs the drink in one, then grimaces. "Gah! That was *not* wine." He turns to me, says "Do you mind?" and takes my glass before I can answer. He downs it. "*That's* better."

Serge Black just nicked my drink. I can only conclude that he is drunk and/or high. Or possibly just a bit of a dick.

*

Pudding
Lionel's Sachertorte

Five missed calls from Mum, seven texts. I sit on the loo listening to her voicemails. The bathroom walls are covered with sheet music instead of wallpaper. I don't recognize any of the songs.

Your aunt Denise is already here and Maggie won't be far behind. Do you know how embarrassing this is?

You'd better call me back, Effie.

I'm serious. Effie, where ARE YOU? I can't believe you're doing this – today of all days. This is so—

Delete. Delete. Sigh and then delete.

Are you at Fran's? Is that where you are? OK … that's it. I'm coming to get you. If you don't call me back in the next ten minutes I swear I'm getting in that car and I will drag you out of that house if I have to.

Shit. I check the time. The message was left eight minutes ago. On the surface of it, it doesn't seem that bad. It's not like she's threatening to call the police or anything. But her turning up at Fran's place? Talking to her, asking her questions. I can't let that happen.

I phone her after I've washed my hands. Just within the ten-minute deadline, but I bet she's already sitting in the car with the engine revving.

It is not a pleasant conversation. I tell her where I am. (*But who ARE these people?*) I make a deal with her. It's my only option.

I have half an hour before she comes to get me. I will go home and I will apologize to everyone. I will smile as they sing 'Happy Birthday' to me and I will open my presents and act suitably grateful for them, and especially grateful for whatever hideous thing Denise has got for me. (*And don't think this means I've forgiven you for this. As soon as everyone's gone we are going to have a serious chat, young lady.*) OK, so she didn't actually say 'young lady', but she may as well have done.

Everyone looks at me when I emerge from the bathroom. Everyone except Serge, who's gone for a nap in AJ's room in an attempt to sober up before tonight. He's supposed to be interviewed live on Radio 6 Music.

"Sorry … I was on the phone. My mum…" I can't bring myself to complete the sentence.

AJ saves me. "You're just in time for the grand finale. Lionel?"

Lionel clambers out of his seat and takes the mystery box off the mantelpiece. He places it on the table and lifts the lid.

Everyone (including me) ooohs and aaahs and just *looks*.

It's the most perfect cake I've ever seen. The top is so glossy I can see my reflection in it. 'Sachertorte' is written on it in impossibly dainty icing.

"Oh, *Lionel*!" says Marjorie. "Dare I say it – even more magnificent than last year!"

Lionel smiles shyly.

I get my phone out to take a picture but AJ shakes his head. "No photos. Lionel's rules. We look, we eat, and then it's gone. Come help me with the plates?"

I follow AJ into the tiny kitchen and Rocky follows me. It's carnage – pots and pans and bowls and chopping boards and baking trays *everywhere*.

"Having fun?" AJ asks as he stretches to reach for some plates on a high shelf.

I nod. "It's…"

"Weird?"

"No!" Because none of it feels weird any more. Not even Lionel's no-pictures rule. "It's brilliant."

"Really?" he asks. "I was a bit worried you might not enjoy it. And that you thought it was weird that I invited you in the first place. I mean, I knew you'd get a kick out of Serge turning up, but it's not like we're really friends or anything, so I wasn't sure if…?"

"I love it. Can I come again next year?"

He laughs. I think he's relieved. "Oh yeah, you've been officially inducted into the Waifs and Strays Hall of Fame now. Attendance is mandatory."

"Suits me just fine."

I don't understand how this boy that I don't even know very well – and these people I've only just met – can make me feel so comfortable. Everything's just *easier* here. AJ may not think that we're friends yet, but I would definitely like to be.

He hands me the plates and directs me to the right drawer for the forks.

I check my watch. "I'm going to have to leave soon…
My mum's coming to pick me up. It's so embarrassing."

"As long as you've got time for cake, it's all good."

I look over my shoulder to check that no one's
listening. "Does he ever speak?"

"He speaks to Marjorie, sometimes."

"What's his deal?"

AJ shrugs. "He's just Lionel."

A shout comes through from the living room.
"Enough dallying in there! It's cake o'clock!" Rocky
thumps his tail on the floor in agreement.

There are so many more questions I want to ask AJ.
I want to know about Serge and why he's here and
what he meant earlier about his life being awful. I
want to know more about Marjorie and Lionel and
AJ's mums. But my questions will have to wait. Cake
comes first.

Lionel cuts the cake and Priya takes a slice through
to the bedroom for Serge. "He's doing better," she says
when she sits back down again.

The Sachertorte is ridiculously good. I have two
helpings and tell Lionel it's the most delicious cake
I have ever tasted. He beams.

Marjorie says that she keeps trying to persuade him to enter *The Great British Bake Off.* Lionel shakes his head and flaps his hand, swatting the idea away.

The doorbell rings and the spell is broken. I jump up to get to the door first and find Mum standing there, car keys in hand. "Come on, let's go."

I turn back to the room and see it through her eyes. Yellow walls, electric blue fireplace, books piled up into precarious towers. The Christmas tree laden with baubles that most definitely do not match, with a grinning Day of the Dead skull on top. This room and the people in it are everything she's not.

"Why don't you come in for a second?" I'm not entirely sure why I say it. To see the look on her face? To delay the inevitably frosty car journey? Or maybe just because I'm not quite ready to leave yet.

For a second I'm sure she's going to say no, but then she arranges a smile on her face and says, "Just for a second."

"This looks very festive," she says when she steps into the room. To her credit, she sounds like she actually means it.

Priya and Sarah are already up out of their seats and

there's a lot of shaking of hands and nice to meet yous. I can't tell if Mum's realized that Sarah and Priya are together, but then Priya kisses Sarah on the cheek when she passes on her way to the kitchen, so she must realize now.

"Jan, would you like a coffee? Or tea? Builder's? Herbal? We have pretty much every type you can think of."

"A small coffee would be lovely, thanks. But then we really must be going." I wait for the pointed glance in my direction, but it never comes. She sits down next to Marjorie and asks how she knows Priya and Sarah, and Marjorie tells her that she's lived three doors down from them since before AJ was born.

I shouldn't be surprised – Mum's always been good at social stuff and small talk. The chatter starts up again, with Sarah joining in and offering Mum some cake. Mum says she really shouldn't, but then she relents and says she'll have a tiny slice with her coffee. Meanwhile I hover awkwardly and wait for her to say something offensive.

Tea and coffee are served in mismatched mugs and Mum says nice things about the cake. She doesn't ask

Lionel if he's got laryngitis and when Serge emerges from the bedroom, sleep-rumpled and looking only slightly less worse for wear than earlier, she takes it in her stride. At least he's sobered up a little. He turns on the charm with Mum and it's the strangest thing to see this musician I've been borderline obsessed with talking about fair-trade coffee with my mother.

I sit on the floor next to the fireplace, sipping peppermint tea from a Darth Vader mug. Priya and Sarah are chatting away with Mum and Marjorie. Lionel's on the sofa with Rocky's head lolling on his lap. AJ's clearing the table so they can play a board game. I'd like to stay and play, although it's probably for the best that I can't. I've been known to get a little over-competitive in the past; like mother, like daughter.

After a few minutes I clamber to my feet. "Come on, Mum. We'd better get going." If Mum can come here and smile and be polite and not act like a douchebag, I think I can manage to do the same back at home.

She looks up, surprised. Pleased, I think. I'm sure she'll still give me a piece of her mind in the car, but I'll take it. She may not understand me and I may not understand her, but perhaps we can find some common ground, somewhere. Maybe we can meet on that common ground every once in a while and have a cup of tea and a biscuit together. I think that would be more than OK.

We say our goodbyes and Serge gives me a hug.

"Welcome to the Club of Lost Souls." So it seems AJ isn't the only one with a nickname for Sarah and Priya's misfit dinner guests. "Sorry about earlier... Listen, AJ tells me you're kind of into my music."

I shoot daggers at AJ, who's looking far too pleased with himself for my liking. I nod, trying to play it cool.

"I could get you on the guest list for my next gig, if you like? You and a friend?"

"That would be... I would *love* that. Thank you."

I think I know just the friend. If she'll take me back.

I get a hug from everyone except Lionel. He doesn't like hugs.

Mum takes Marjorie's number. It seems they've discovered a mutual love of theatre.

I thank Sarah and Priya for the meal and say that I hope I'll see them again soon. Sarah gives me a Tupperware box and Priya squeezes my arm and says,

"Feel free to drop by whenever. Our home is your home." I smile shyly and then she says, "I mean it, Effie."

I know she does.

The Associates

*

Kevin Brooks

"I'm like a bird."

Manny and Hugh are perched on the second-from-top step outside the library, their knees drawn up and their shoulders hunched against the cold. A never-ending stream of mid-morning traffic coils back and forth along the narrow high street in front of them, filling the wintry air with a constant rumble and a blue-grey choke of exhaust fumes.

Hugh cups a grimy hand around his cigarette lighter, trying to light the dead stub of a roll-up hanging from his lip.

"What?" he says to Manny.

"I'm like a bird," Manny repeats.

"What kind of bird?"

Manny flicks his head back, rearranging a loose twist of long black hair. "No kind. Just a bird."

The two men lapse into a comfortable silence – Manny browsing idly through his library book (*The A–Z of Serial Killers*), while Hugh just sits there watching the world go by. He watches an old lady scuttling along the pavement, dragging a wheeled shopping trolley behind her. He watches (and listens) as a whistling van driver slams his rear doors shut, then whistles his way round to the front of the van, gets in and starts the engine. And he watches a young woman with drug-haunted eyes buying cheap cuts of meat in the butcher's shop across the road.

"See him?" he says to Manny after a while.

Manny looks up from his book and sees a teenage boy with a rock-hard slab of heavily gelled hair slouching past the library steps.

"Hey, kid!" Hugh calls out. "Where d'you get the hat?"

The boy glances anxiously at the two grubby men on the steps, his hand rising instinctively towards his head. He doesn't know what Hugh means – what hat? – or if the two men mean him any harm or not. Hugh and Manny don't help him out, they just sit there staring blankly at him. The boy lowers his hand, looks away, and self-consciously walks on by.

Hugh pulls hard on the half-inch stub of his cigarette, hoping for a final hit, but there's nothing left of it now. He takes it from his mouth, gives it a disapproving look, then flicks it away. He sticks his hands into the warmth of his coat pockets, automatically feeling (and recognizing) their contents – fluff, bits of a lolly stick, tobacco dust … penknife, string, an unknown key … a partly sucked boiled sweet (coated with fluff and tobacco dust), a pencil stub, tobacco tin…

Across the road, next to the butcher's, a young couple are looking at the houses for sale in an estate agent's window. The man is tall and blond, and dressed in a pristine white rugby shirt. His partner – wife? girlfriend? – has perfectly groomed light brown hair and is wearing an unseasonably short dress that leaves little to the imagination.

Hugh stares at her backside, imagining a parallel universe in which he's the one looking at houses in an estate agent's window, dressed in a pristine white rugby shirt, with his pretty young wife standing beside him in an unseasonably short dress that draws the attention of two grubby men sitting on the steps outside the library across the road…

The man turns round then, and when he sees Hugh staring at his wife's/girlfriend's backside, he narrows his eyes and gives him a tough-guy glare.

Hugh sets the mark of the devil into his face and stares right back, and a moment later the man takes his wife/girlfriend by the arm and moves on.

"Hair, stare, glare, scare," says Hugh.

"She was there," adds Manny, "showing off her underwear."

A lorry shudders to a halt outside the pet shop on the corner. As the airbrakes let out a weary sigh, the driver takes a sheet of paper from his pocket, unfolds it and reads. He frowns for a second or two, scratching his head, then he drops the paper on the seat beside him, puts the lorry into gear, and rumbles off again.

In the pet shop, a woman in glasses is sitting on a stool next to the till, filling mesh bags with peanuts.

The two men sit for a while longer – reading, smoking, sniffing, coughing … watching the December day unravel.

Sometime later, the town hall clock strikes twelve.

"Ready?" says Hugh.

"Yep," says Manny.

They stand up, slap the dust from their trousers, and set off up the high street. They walk side by side, with unconcerned ease, like two indomitable cowboys, Dusty and Slim, moseying on up to the bunkhouse after a hard morning's work.

*

This town is known for its swans. They gather at the side of a long straight road that runs alongside the estuary. Visitors from out of town stop their cars, buy ice creams from ice-cream vans and feed the swans. They feed them on bread, crisps, buns, ice cream, nuts and chocolate bars, but the swans remain as white as the morning snow. Manny and Hugh neither like nor dislike them. They're just there, like everything else.

The two companions dine at Gino's. Or, to be more accurate, they buy their fish and chips from Gino's and dine on them across the road on a bench beneath the War Memorial.

Hugh leans his head back, gazing up at the list of names inscribed on the marble monolith above him. Still leaning back, he drops a vinegar-soaked chip into his mouth and chews it slowly.

"They didn't exactly *give* their lives for their country, did they?" he says, the chip steam rising from his mouth.

Manny picks pieces of skin from a saveloy and throws them into the gutter. He bites into the skinless meat and watches sparrows and pigeons vying for the scraps.

It's getting colder now.

When Manny had said he was like a bird, he was referring specifically – if somewhat obliquely – to his total inability to recognize or understand numbers. The prices on Gino's menu board, for example, mean absolutely nothing to him:

Cod – squiggle.

Saveloy – squiggle.

Chips – squiggle.

He gets by though, like a bird gets by. And Hugh's always there for him. Always.

Manny holds a steaming fat chip to his mouth and blows on it. The smell of hot vinegar waltzes drunkenly in the winter air.

"Lil might be there tonight," says Hugh, spitting out a sliver of fish bone.

Tonight is the Christmas dinner at the community centre for the elderly and disadvantaged.

"Fat Lil," muses Manny.

"Not so fat."

"Fat enough."

"For what?"

Manny doesn't reply. He screws up his chip paper into a ball and lobs it into a wire-mesh bin.

"You'll be shaving, then?" he says to Hugh.

Hugh shakes his head. "Lil likes a beard."

"So she does."

Hugh rolls a cigarette and belches quietly. He steals a reverent glance at Manny, unaware of himself digging his thumbnail deep into the soft wet wood of the bench.

Does he love him?

No one shall ever know anything of that: only he and I and a tiny little bird, Tandaraday! who will never let fall a word.

*

It's late afternoon now, the pale winter sun beginning to set, and Manny and Hugh are heading home.

They move, as ever, at no great pace. Along Station Road, past the flat greyness of the industrial estate, under the railway bridge, past the high-pitched drilling of A1 Auto Services, over the roundabout by the railway station, and on up the hill, on the road out of town.

"You know what I'd like?" says Hugh.

"What?" says Manny, swaying away from the downhill rush of a container lorry.

"A map of the world."

They stop at a gap in the hedge and lean together over a five-bar metal gate, looking out across the uphill slope of a barren field.

"Where's all the sheep gone?" says Manny.

"Chopped up for dinners," says Hugh.

They climb the gate.

As Manny swings a tattered trouser leg over the top bar, a woman cleaning her bedroom window in a house across the road catches a brief glimpse of off-white vagabond pants.

"*Oof!*" she says.

Manny and Hugh hike their way up the field. A woodpecker bobs across the sky and disappears into its tree, laughing as it goes. Hugh pauses, breaking into a violent fit of coughing. Doubled over, hands on knees, he hawks and hacks until eventually the coughing stops. He spits a final gob, wipes his mouth with his sleeve, then gingerly straightens up.

"All right?" Manny says softly.

Hugh nods.

As they carry on up the slope, the dilapidated wire-mesh fence at the top of the hill draws closer. Beyond it lies their home – a derelict mansion house. There's not much left of the once-grand building. Anything of value has long since been wrecked or stripped away – glass, tiles, lead, stonework – and all that's left now is a desolate shell. The roof has gone – the few remaining broken timbers jutting out like ancient yellowed bones – and the crumbling stone walls are holed with glassless windows. A hundred years ago, the courtyard in front of the house would have hosted splendid garden parties for the privileged few, but now it's just a cracked and weed-infested concrete square strewn with rubble and waste – empty beer cans and cider bottles, used syringes, shredded carrier bags, the desiccated remains of long-dead animals...

It's a place that reeks of fallen grace. From a mansion house to a tuberculosis sanatorium during the war, from a sanatorium to an industrial plastics factory in the eighties, and now, in its senility, the house has once more become a home.

And as Manny and Hugh cross the courtyard together, the empty black eyes of the derelict building look down on them, welcoming them back at the end of their day.

The Afterschool Club

*

Holly Bourne

We were from different worlds.

That's how these stories always start, isn't it?

This isn't that kind of story.

We were though.

Ben was glitter, I was dust. Ben was golden, I was grey. Ben ruled the school, I ruled the scruffy patch of weeds behind the astroturf. Ben scored goals, I scored weed. Ben wore the latest football boots, I coloured in the worn patches of my biker boots with permanent marker. Ben was one of Them, I was never truly one of anything. Ben smiled, I scowled. Ben ruled, I rebelled.

We never spoke during the day.

But he would always meet me at 4.45 p.m., on the wall.

"You all right, Mercedes?" He appeared out of the darkness, spinning a football on his finger, and sat down next to me. "How was noise practice?"

I flicked the ball. It bounced and he caught it expertly. "Band practice was fine, thank you. How was the-pointless-kicking-of-a-ball-around-a-square?"

He laughed, a snort of it, and spun the ball again. "It was great, thank you. We won."

"Won what?"

"The game, durr."

"Didn't anyone tell you it's not the winning, but the taking part that counts?"

Another snort of laughter and he grinned. Ben's grin could melt most people. But I wasn't most people. Well, I didn't want him to think I was. That would ruin everything.

"That's what losers say," Ben said.

"You splitting the world into winners and losers, now?"

The smile stretched wider, my insides melted further. I gulped it down.

"Around you, Miss Angry?" he said. "I wouldn't dare."

*

We walked the back way into town, like always – taking the shortcut through the scrubby woods, getting mud on our shoes. A hanging bit of branch got stuck in my hair and pulled me back with a snap. I twisted to try and get it off, but my scalp complained as it pulled harder.

"Ouch." I glowed, mortified.

Ben stopped, laughed, and turned to help me untangle it.

"Stop struggling, you're making it worse," he said.

I held still dumbly, not sure how to act with his face so close to mine. He smelled amazing – of expensive aftershave and clean after the shower. "Wow. It's proper stuck. This tree really likes you."

I wiggled, my scalp twinging in pain as my hair tangled further. "Can you get it out?" I had nightmare visions of him having to leave me here to go get scissors.

"Yes, hold still though. You're making it worse. God, your hair is SO long."

I closed my eyes for a moment to block the view of him so close, to block how it made me feel. Could he see the caking of my cheap foundation around my nose? Would he notice the beige bumps on my chin where concealer was covering the cluster of spots that took up camp there a year ago and wouldn't leave? Was he comparing my grey, flaky face to the perfect pore-free skin of the girls he normally hangs out with? Girls like Jenny Carrington, whose pricey foundation floats flawlessly on to her glowing kale-eating skin. I heard he made out with her at Danny's party last month... The sort of gossip that trickles down to even the social dredges like me.

I opened my eyes and found his. They were hazel, big, as he stared at my face with intense concentration. His fingers fumbled clumsily with my hair – probably making it worse. I remembered one evening last year, before my big brother, Alfie, left us. He'd said he didn't think plaiting hair was hard, so I'd tried to teach him. It was like a gorilla trying to figure out how to play violin or something.

"Got it!" Ben announced triumphantly. "You're free."

"Thanks." I felt the distance between us the moment he stepped away.

*

We went to McDonald's. We ordered what we always order. Ben paid like he always paid. He provides the fast food, I provide the dazzling entertainment... Ha. And the vodka. Or gin. Or whisky. Or cider. Whatever I occasionally steal without my stepdad noticing. We sat in our corner booth and ate. He had two double cheeseburgers, fries and a strawberry shake. I had a Happy Meal, still compensating for all the Happy Meals I never got as a kid.

"You get a good toy?" He pointed to my bright cardboard box and I could see the meat in his mouth as he talked.

I tipped the box over and a neon pink pony fell out. "Just a heavily gendered plastic horse," I replied.

Ben rolled his eyes. "Always a conspiracy with you, isn't there?"

I nodded and took a slurp of my chocolate milkshake. "Always." But when he wasn't looking, I tucked the pony into my coat pocket for Natalia. She would love it. I could maybe even save it for Christmas, give it to her as a present. Just in case Mum and my stepdad forgot.

I pointed to Ben's milkshake. "Strawberry?"

He sighed. "And what's wrong with strawberry?"

"It's just pink, that's all."

He grinned his grin, bit the straw. "And you were just about to go off on a gender rant… Hypocrite."

I smiled back, despite myself. "But would you order strawberry if your football mates were here?"

"As a matter of fact, I would."

"Well, that's told me, hasn't it?"

He took another slurp, reached for a cluster of fries and folded them between his white teeth. "Tell me, Mercedes, is there any part of the universe you don't want to start a fight with?"

I used my milkshake cup to toast him. "Is there any part of the universe you don't want to charm?"

"There's nothing wrong with being friendly."

"There's nothing wrong with calling an arse an arse."

"Isn't it supposed to be a spade?"

"I prefer arse."

He raised his eyebrows at that, and smirked. "I'll keep that in mind."

"Oh, for God's sake, you're such a LAD!" And I

chucked a chip at him. It landed right on his forehead and ricocheted on to the floor.

"I deserved that," he agreed. Still holding eye contact, still smirking.

And I thought, *Are you thinking of me like that? In a nice way? Do I ever cross your mind when I'm not there? Do you ever wonder what I'm doing when we ignore each other at school? Like I do with you.*

Ben looked away, a tiny bit of red rising up from underneath his polo shirt. He pointed out the steamy window to our nondescript high street. "It's snowing."

My eyes followed his finger. "Bollocks."

"I know."

It was only a flurry, the odd flake tumbling out of the sky and melting on the chewing-gum-laden pavement. I shivered in anticipation, even though we were right under the heating unit. It wasn't time for us to go to the park yet. We didn't go until at least eight.

Ben stood up, stretched. "I'll get more chips."

I watched people's eyes following him as he walked to the counter. A diamond in the rough-side-of-town. A nugget of gold in the silt.

I was the silt.

Their eyes went from him to me. I looked into the cup, taking off the top so I could stir the shake with my straw. I knew what they were thinking. *Why is a guy like that with a girl like her?* I put my finger over the top of my straw, lifted it out of the shake, then released my finger so the liquid dropped back down. I looked out of the window at the people bracing themselves against the cold, leaning into the wind.

We were going to freeze later.

A bag of fries skidded to a halt in front of me. "Your chips, madam." Ben bowed.

I smiled and saluted. "Why, thank you, kind sir."

"You're supposed to curtsey to a bow, not salute," he complained, sliding back into the booth and reaching for a handful of fries.

"Um, Ben? Look at me." I pointed at myself. "My name is Mercedes, for fuck's sake – let's not pretend I'll ever be someone who curtseys."

It came out harsher than I meant it to, inflating the air with awkward. It was like that a lot with us. Loaded silences more frequent than trains at rush hour. Always weighing up the other's comments. *Can I trust you to keep our secret? About what we do together?*

It was him who diffused the tension. It always was.

"You've got such a chip on your shoulder." He reached over and put an actual French fry on my shoulder.

I smiled, getting a whiff of his smell. "Naffest. Joke. Ever."

"Says the person who just used the word 'naff'?"

"Naff is a naff word?"

"Naff is the naffest of all the words. Only naff people use the word naff."

I plucked the chip off and ate it, the salt burning my tongue.

"I can't believe you just *ate* the chip on your shoulder. Does that mean you'll stop teasing me about my trainers?"

I looked pointedly down at his trainers peeking out beneath the table. The latest Nikes, still mostly fresh and white from the box. The sort of trainers that would feed Mum, me and Natalia for a month. Not that you can eat trainers…

"I'll stop teasing you about your trainers, the day you stop wearing trainers that define everything that is wrong with this world."

He rolled his eyes, but he was smiling. Maybe that's

what you need to be golden, to glow like Ben glowed – effortless good humour.

"Everything that's wrong with this world?"

I nodded.

"What about famine? Or disease? Or global warming? Or antibiotic resistance?"

I pulled a face. "How do you know about antibiotic resistance?"

"Biology homework... Actually, that reminds me. I've got to do some."

"Swot."

"Stoner." He rummaged in his bag and got out his books, opening a textbook to a page about panda breeding cycles.

Stoner? I'll show him. I got out my music coursework and spread all my stuff out, deliberately taking up more than my half of the table. He rolled his eyes again. Smiling again.

We worked and ate chips, dipping them into both our milkshakes. Sometimes I looked up and watched him work. He did this thing with his tongue when he concentrated that I found kind of mesmerizing, rolling it into his cheek.

Once, when I glanced at him, I caught him doing the same. We both turned red and looked back down at our papers. His expression hadn't been admiring though ... more puzzled, like I was an equation he was trying to solve.

I finished my music essay and moved on to my maths homework. Ben was good for my GCSEs, that was for sure. I never used to do work – never used to see the point. But since we'd been coming to McDonald's, I did it because he was doing it and it would be weird if I just ... I dunno ... stared at him.

But soon the chips ran out. The place had got busy. People stood with laden trays, eyeing our empty ones with furrowed brows. It was time to go.

"Ready, camper?" Ben asked, packing his stuff away.

I pointed out of the window to the snowflakes swirling under the orange glow of the streetlights. "It's still snowing," I said, stating the obvious.

"Shit." He so rarely swore and I jumped. "It's going to be freezing. You brought ... you know?"

"Yep. I've been saving this bottle, to celebrate the almost-end of term."

"Well, that will help, I suppose."

*

It was knock-the-breath-out-of-you cold as we emerged, pulling our coats around us, Ben shoving on his famous bobble hat. We didn't mention the cold, we didn't complain. We were dedicated to what this was. We walked, wordlessly, to the park. I glanced at my phone, it was half eight. We'd managed to eke out our McDonald's section of the evening for half an hour longer than usual. I had a few messages from the band.

Today was sic —Mandy

I've got a boner just thinking about how good we sounded —Pete

I smiled and tried to type back, but my hands were too cold and I gave up after misspelling the first word four times.

At least Ben had a proper coat, I thought bitterly. It was a Barbour. Ben was the only boy I knew who could pull off a Barbour. It was one of those quilted ones and it looked so warm. When he'd come in with it after half-term, he'd been mocked for ten whole minutes and called a farmer. The next week, half the school were wearing cheap rip-offs. As if he could sense my anger, Ben turned to me just as we got to the park entrance.

"You want to switch coats? You look freezing."

I shook my head, even though it killed me to do it. "I'm good. You can't pull off leather anyway, Posh Boy." My body screamed as I said it, yelling, *Noooooooo, take the coat, take the coat.*

"At least take my hat." He pulled off his bobble hat and yanked it down over my head without asking. It pushed my fringe down into my eyes.

"And now I look stupid," I said. When all I really wanted to say was *thank you*.

"I don't care. Your lips are blue. You're wearing it."

The park was pitch black, even the post-commute dog walkers in for the night. We walked using the light from our phones to guide the way, though we knew it by heart.

I dawdled after him, blinking hard, feeling … wrong, like I always do whenever anyone shows me just a hint of caring, even if it's just Golden Ben saying I look cold.

I don't know how to handle people caring about me.

So I reached into my pocket and I got out the poached vodka.

I unscrewed the cap, noticing only a third of it had gone already and hoping my stepdad hadn't been too sober when he hid it in the tiny cupboard under the stairs. I wouldn't want him to notice it missing... I'd stolen it a few days ago though and he hadn't mentioned anything. And I would KNOW if he had. I threw back my head, tipped some down my neck, swallowed, winced. "Want any?" I held out the bottle in the darkness between us.

"I'll wait until *after* I've vaulted the railing, thanks."

"You have to vault the railings on the way out anyway."

"Yes, well, I only want a fifty per cent chance of spearing myself through the heart rather than a hundred per cent."

When we got to the railings, Ben squatted, with both hands cradled on his thigh.

"Cheers." I put my hands on his shoulder and stepped my boot into his cupped hands. I swung myself up, grabbing the railings.

This part of the night always made my heart thud. The closeness of us touching. Our skin brushing as I shimmied up and over the railings.

Ben didn't need a leg-up – the sports god that he was. He used the railings to do a chin-up, his arms bulging as he raised himself up and threw his body over.

We landed together on the bouncy red tarmac with a light thud.

"We're in." He held out his hand for the vodka bottle.

"We're in." I handed it over.

And we made our way to the playhouse.

*

The playhouse was under a concrete tunnel thing, adding extra layers against the cold. It was where we'd first met. Well, 'met' as in actually acknowledging the other's existence for the first time, without school and all the bullshit barriers school creates between two people who may have otherwise got along. He'd found me crying and drunk two months ago. I remember, even through my intoxication, being surprised that he knew who I was. I'd never been here in daylight. Natalia had been taken away before she was old enough to come. I'd never seen it with children inside, playing cooking or mums and dads or whatever kids play, not realizing just how lucky they are not to be grown-up yet. Not that I was even grown-up yet.

My teeth chattered as we sat inside, our knees hunched up, passing the vodka bottle back and forth. They clacked in my mouth, my jaw juddering uncontrollably.

"Oh, for Christ's sake, Mercedes."

"Huh?"

I turned and Ben was up, shrugging off his coat, holding it out to me.

"I'm fine," I insisted, though it came out. *"I'm f-ii-ii-ii-nn-ee."*

He tilted his head and let out a breath of exasperation. "Can you not be too proud for, like, one evening?"

My face jerked back. Too proud? I wasn't too proud ... was I? Then why wasn't I taking his coat? He pushed it at me again.

"Honestly, I've got my football hoodie in my bag. I'll be OK. You, on the other hand, look almost purple."

I relented and took his coat. Nobody had ever given me their coat before. The cold rushed all over my body as I shrugged out of my battered leather jacket. But as I wrapped Ben's around me, I warmed instantly.

It still had his body heat inside it, like he was hugging me. Like I was being wrapped in a radiator. Ben pulled on a big jumper. His T-shirt rode up as he pushed his head through the neck and I made myself look away.

I held out my dishevelled jacket. "You want?"

"I'll look ridiculous."

"I won't tell anyone."

He smiled, took it, and tried to squeeze his big sporty arms into it. He did look ridiculous. It hardly fitted him, stretching across his back and making him look like Quasimodo – his arms hanging uselessly at his sides. I started laughing and then, because the vodka was starting to hit, I laughed harder. I took a photo of him on my phone while he posed. When I showed it to him he said, "Dear God," but kept the jacket on. Then he stayed looking at my phone, his face so close our breath mingled, and I knew what he wanted. So I deleted the photo and felt him relax.

No evidence.

We leaned back against the wood panelling, getting drunk and watching the snow.

*

"It's settling," I said.

I was no longer cold. I was vodka.

I dug in my bag for cigarettes, shoved one into my mouth and lit it. I offered the pack to Ben, he declined.

"I love that word, 'settling', and how they use it for snow," he mused. "Like the snow aspired to much better things than just landing here."

I took a drag, smiling, and put on a silly squeaky voice. "I used to dream about falling in Iceland, you know? But then I hit thirty and all my other snowflake friends settled here and I just … I dunno what happened… Life happened. So I settled here."

We both giggled in the darkness.

"You think we'll get a snow day tomorrow?" he asked, staring out at the primary-coloured tarmac speckled with white.

Just the thought of it made my stomach tighten. A day … a whole day to fill. And the holidays were almost here, too. So many days to fill… I shook my head, like the force of my will could change the weather. My laughter died inside of me and was replaced by dread.

"God, let's hope not."

I took another drag, exhaled, and watched my smoke

drift out into the night. I could feel Ben watching me.

"Why do you smoke?" he asked, all of a sudden.

I shrugged. "I dunno. I just do."

"And weed. You smoke a lot of weed, too, don't you?"

Another shrug. "I guess."

"Why?"

My lip curled. "I told you. I don't know. I just do…"
It's what all my friends did, I never thought to question
it. I bumped my shoulder with his. "Come on, Mr
Judgemental, it's not like you're so perfect. I hear what
you and your lot get up to at your rich-people parties."

There were stories of skinny-dipping in swimming
pools, stories of trashed golfing buggies, stories of
orgy-like states, nobody sure who was in whose
mouth. Shots and blazers and ruddy-ruddy-rah-rahs
and bending each other over and slapping each other's
arses and drinking until they vomited and then frying
their vomit into an omelette and being dared to eat it.

"I told you eight million times," he sighed. "I'm
not rich … not any more." Which is why he started
at our school, he'd once told me. Because his parents
could no longer afford the fees. He could still afford
new trainers and McDonald's and to escape this town

eventually though. "Anyway," he continued, "what we do isn't illegal, but drugs are." His voice was groaning under the weight of his judgement.

My stomach twisted in on itself. "Nothing people from your world do is ever illegal," I replied. "That's the difference between rich and poor. Your trouble is *oops-sorry-slap-on-the-wrist, we-won't-do-it-again-sir,* and our trouble is *shove-you-in-an-overcrowded-prison.*" I was sucking too hard on my cigarette to curb my anger, waving it in the air as I ranted.

"Whoa, OK. Calm down..." He eyed me warily and I levelled him with my best glare. I looked at his smooth skin and his perfectly cut hair, I looked at his expensive bag, his clean trainers, his easier life. People think I'm thick – I know that. They see me slumping through lessons, high in the afternoons. They see my long hair and my bad friends and our silly band and the cheap uniform you have to get in a special charity sale and they make assumptions. But I'm not stupid. I read. I know what's going on in the world. I know that it's the actions of people like Ben and his lot that led to Mum's benefit getting cut and my stepdad losing his job at the pub. Cause and effect. The butterfly effect. And, yeah, oh, poor fucking Ben, he can't go to Arlington Grammar any more, but I got my SISTER taken away. And yet, *they* judge *us*. Ben judges me.

I stood up.

"Where you going?"

"Away." My voice slurred, with drink and almost-tears.

"It's freezing out there."

I stormed off anyway, into the playground. I felt so ... so... The snow scrunched under my boots as I stomped over to the swings, sweeping the snow off one. I sat down, leaned my head against the chain and let myself cry. It wasn't fair, none of it.

I heard the crunch of his footsteps, the clank of the chain on the swing next to me as he sat down. He said, "I'm sorry."

I sniffed. "You think you're better than me."

"Whoa, I don't! Where the hell is this coming from?"

The snow melted on my hair, freezing my brain, but I hardly noticed. I looked over at him. He was still wearing my leather jacket. "You don't even want people to know about me," I said, watching his reaction, looking for tells that he was lying.

"No, I don't. I don't want people to know that I come here," he admitted. He didn't look back, just straight out into the darkness, where the slide was.

"See!" I acted triumphant, but my heart plunged to the tips of my frozen toes.

"Hang on, but that doesn't mean I think I'm better than you!" He did look at me then, eyes wide with protest. "It's not about you, Mercedes. Being here with you. I'm not ashamed of you…"

"But…" I waited for the backpedal, the silly excuse. My face was burning red, even in this cold. Whatever this was, I was breaking it. Which is stupid, because I needed it. We both needed it. It's why we kept coming. We had no other choice.

He sighed and threw his arms up, pushed himself back with his legs and let himself swing. "It's really not about you," he said. "I just don't want people knowing about any of it. About why I need to come here. Asking questions. Wanting answers. I don't like to think about what's going on and how messed up it is, let alone talk about it. Try and explain it away, like my mother does." He skidded himself to a halt, his feet scuffing in the small pile of snow. He looked at me;

smiled. "To be fair, you're probably the only good thing about all this."

He pushed his legs to the right, so his swing moved toward mine – his body looming closer. I could feel the warmth from him.

Was he playing me? Lying to me? Soothing me so I'd shut up?

I raised an eyebrow at him. "Yeah, right…"

"Seriously."

If he was playing me, he was good at this game. Every inch of his body bled sincerity. I found my own swing creeping in his direction, my body pushing itself to his, because it's never known what's good for me.

"Even though I'm a down-and-out mess?"

He shook his head ever so slightly. "That's the thing. That's why I asked about your smoking. You're not," he replied. "How you behave … from what I've learned about you … you're not that at all. It doesn't make sense."

"Well, you don't make a lot of sense either."

Because he didn't. Ben didn't lend coats, Ben didn't untangle hair, Ben didn't pay for a random girl's McDonald's, night after night. Ben beat his chest and everyone cheered. Ben said the word 'banter'. Ben winked at Jenny Carrington as she sauntered down the hallway. Ben, sometimes, walked past my friends and sniggered.

Our heads were almost touching, our bodies twisted in chains and we leaned in to each other. It would only take one movement and we would be kissing. I looked up at him through my lashes, wanting ... thinking... I could tell he wanted it. I could see it in his eyes, feel it in his energy. The way he looked nervous, the way he licked his lip without realizing, the way his hand shook on the chain, and not just because it was cold. I wanted it, too. Of course I did. Every girl in school wanted Ben. But I didn't want the Ben everyone at school got. I wanted the Ben only I knew. The Ben who gave me leg-ups over railings, the Ben who, last month, stayed out all night with me without even asking why. The Ben who, last week, turned up at our meeting spot with a giant bag of pick 'n' mix and told me his favourites were jazzies. I wanted the taste of Ben in my mouth, the feel of his hands at the back of my neck.

Ben looked at me, I looked at Ben. I blinked away snowflakes. We leant closer ... closer...

...

...We both pulled back at exactly the same moment.

Then we kicked ourselves into our swings, like it had never happened at all.

Freezing air sailed past me as I pumped my legs through snow and blackness. That feeling of freedom and flying as I swung through the air, Ben at my side.

"You ever think of getting out of here?" he called over. He was swinging back as I swung forward, meeting in the middle each time.

I laughed to diffuse the tension we were currently swinging through. "How?"

"Go to university. Get a loan or something."

I laughed again. "Not going to happen."

I would finish school the moment I was legally allowed to, so I could earn money and escape. I would get one of the shit jobs they give people who leave school the moment they are legally allowed to. I would harden before my time, always struggle to make rent, always have a chip right there on my shoulder. It was my path and I felt powerless to stop it. The thought of doing anything else was too exhausting. My only real hope was that they might let me have Natalia, if I could earn enough. If I could prove I'd give her a better home.

"What about your singing?" he asked. "I heard you at the talent show last year, you're really good."

I almost skidded to a stop. *He'd heard me?*

I did dream about singing. The only time I felt free was with my band, a mic in my hand, an audience clapping.

"Your band are terrible though," he continued. "You should take off on your own. Write your own stuff maybe..."

I was too stunned to reply for a moment, until I just lobbed, "Shut up, Yoko," at him. He laughed, surprising me by getting the joke. I had thought about it. I'd even been tempted to enter that bloody singing show on TV, but my friends would kill me. Laugh at me. Tell me I'd sold out.

"It's OK for you," I say. "What have you got? Two and a bit more years? Then off to university with you. Your escape tunnel has already been dug."

...And paid for.

But when I looked over, he wasn't smiling.

"Hardly an escape tunnel," he replied. "Going to the university my parents choose, doing the course they want me to do."

"Aww, diddums." At least it was university. Options. Choice. Not this town…

"You don't get it," he said.

"Well, you don't get it either."

He skidded his swing to a halt, the chain screeching in protest. "Let's stop trying to get it and finish the vodka."

*

It's hard, vaulting iron railings after a bottle of vodka. But we giggled and we tried and we managed. We stumbled back through the park, deliberately walking wider and narrower again, leaving as many footprints in the snow as we could.

I exist. I was here. I walked here. Here is a piece of me. A piece of me to prove I'm alive.

I walked him to his house – it was always that way around.

"So what's your excuse for tonight?" I asked.

Ben made himself skid on some ice. "I'm chairperson of this year's Rag Ball, don't you know? We have lots of meetings. An infinite amount of meetings." He smiled sadly. "What's yours?"

"I never need one. We're both equally glad when I'm not there."

There was space between each house in this neighbourhood. And it was so quiet. Just us and the snow. There was no tinny music, no noise from other people's televisions, no barking dogs in tiny gardens, or shouting and crashing the whole road would wince at, then pretend they hadn't heard. Not like that didn't happen in this road, too – you just didn't hear it, I suppose.

We never usually talked on the walk back. Tension would build inside of us as we worried if we'd stayed out late enough, stayed out long enough. For our houses to find sleep, so we could slip in and pretend they were homes.

I skidded as we stopped outside Ben's house. We both looked up at it blearily. It was dark, all lights off, and I felt his relief. He sank into his bones, let go of the breath he'd been holding. Whatever he'd wanted to avoid so much he'd freeze to death in my leather jacket, he'd successfully delayed.

For one more night at least.

"Looks all clear," I whispered – just in case my voice could travel through their double glazing and undo the spell.

"Seems that way."

"I guess I'll see you, then."

"Tomorrow?"

"Tomorrow. Last day of term..."

We swapped back coats, it breaking my heart and my body temperature to part with his.

"Thank you, for lending it."

"Any time."

He turned and crunched through the snow – on a slight tiptoe to minimise noise. He stopped for a second, turned back.

"You going to be OK?" His voice was filled with concern.

I looked at the time on my phone. We'd made it till 11.30. "I should be fine."

"You've got my number if it isn't fine?"

I bit my lip. "I've got it."

"Well, night, then."

"Night."

"Mercedes?" he called after me in a loud whisper as I was almost past his house. He blinked hard, his fists clenched. "Honestly," he stumbled. "If you need to call me tonight, do. My phone's always on."

"Ditto for you." And I saluted.

The snow had almost stopped, but enough of it swirled around us as we stood and smiled at each other. Distance between us, but not the sort that counted. Different worlds, but the same sad reality. And I wish I could freeze-frame on that moment, with the snowflakes and Ben's dimples and my body still warm from his coat. The two of us not knowing yet that I hadn't stayed out late enough, that I *would* need to call him later, screaming for help down the line. But that moment wasn't now. That reality was yet to exist.

So, if we end here, we can say this is a happy ending. Can't we?

Homo for Christmas

*

Juno Dawson

Is there anything more repulsive than people eating crisps on trains? I watch a businessman shovel greasy pawfuls of salt and vinegar Tyrrells into his gob, crumbs raining down on to his moobs. They reek, too, and he's on his second gin-in-a-tin. He's watching *Mad Men* on an iPad and looks like he's hankering to go back to the good old days when you could smoke in the office and slap women on the arse as they walk by.

I've got that 'Driving Home for Christmas' song stuck in my head on loop even though, technically, I'm not. It's Christmas Eve Eve Eve and the train is packed. I had to ask Crisp Man to move his briefcase off my seat and he wasn't happy about it. I asked if his briefcase had bought its own ticket. He didn't like that either.

Never mind crisps, I'm too nervous to eat. I can't even stomach a cup of tea.

I rub my sweaty palms on my jeans and try to focus on my essay. Something about ethics in psychology. The Milgram Experiment and Skinner and all that. I'm still not sure about psychology. One semester in and it's not the *Criminal Minds* stuff I thought it would be. I've already asked, and I can switch to criminology before second year if I want to without having to start over.

A new thought butts in: This could be the last time I sit on a train to Newcastle.

My heart is proper achy.

As if he can sense me having a wobble, my phone lights up and it's Ade. I swipe into the message.

Hi McSexface! You don't have to do anything if it doesn't feel right x

I want to, I reply. And I do. Well, I don't, but I have to, like.

The crazy thing is, all I have to do is think about Ade and it chills me out. I think about him making up a little song this morning called 'You Have to Get In the Shower Now Or You'll Be Late But You Should Definitely Make Me a Cup of Tea First', and singing it in my ear as we were squidged like sardines in his single bed. I smile to myself.

We usually sleep at his halls, as my cell is right next to the lift and it clanks and whirrs all night. His always smells of pot, but at least it's quiet and warm. He's in the posh halls, I'm in the povo ones.

I so wish he were with me for our first Christmas together. We've barely spent a night apart since Halloween and my big bed at home is gonna be bloody Baltic without him in it.

Although it will be quite nice to kick my legs around.

This is why I'm doing it. This is why I *have* to tell her – because then, the next time I come home, I can bring Ade with me.

My stomach gurgles again. I picture green, toxic, nervous gunk churning around inside me. I remember a few years back when we had *Hollyoaks* on at home and John Paul tashed on with Ste, and Mam was like, "Ooh do we have to see that while we're eating our tea?". It was steak and kidney pie, mash and mushy peas. I still remember.

At the time, I was jealous of Ste, I just didn't know it. It was like someone trying to explain a rhino to someone who's never seen one. It didn't make a lot of sense. I hadn't joined the dots.

I'm a good-looking lad (not to mention *very* humble). I'm told I'm the spit of my dad and that's probably why Mam sometimes looks like she wants to knock me teeth out. I don't remember him, if I'm honest. Girls loved me at school. I was called Hunky Dunc – and didn't I just love that.

I loved girls… Well, girl, singular. Me and Ellie were together since Year 11 and I thought I was proper in love with her. Well, I was, just not the same kind of love I'm falling into now. It's what you do, isn't it? I was on the football team, had all my own teeth and a four-pack if not a six-pack. I'm a tidy specimen. Everyone else was tashing on with girls, so I did, too.

Maybe I'm, like, bi or something, because when I had sex with Ellie it wasn't repulsive or anything. It was nice. But it was nice like eating cornflakes. These days I'm strictly on Coco Pops. Shit, is that racist? Ade's skin is actually the colour of Coco Pops milk now I think about it. Balls, I just meant I'm now on a superior breakfast cereal, which Coco Pops clearly is.

Ade wasn't the first guy I mucked about with either. Fernando.

OK, I don't actually know if his name was Fernando,

that's just what I've christened him. In the Easter holidays of Year 12, a few of us decided to have a lads' holiday to Kavos. It was mint. Gaz got so sunburnt on the first day, he had to lurk in the shadows like a mardy vampire for the rest of the week. Every night we went out, had a skinful and got slaughtered; slept till eleven or twelve and then hit the beach.

Near the end of the week, we was on the beach. The sun was starting to set and it wasn't quite so roasting. I was cooling off in the sea on my own when I first saw him. He had a cracking body – just wearing a pair of turquoise Speedos – proper six-pack and tattoos. Definitely foreign … lush olive skin. Maybe I've got a type.

He clocked us and sorta gave us a nod. I just looked away and dived under the water. I swam it off. How did he know? Did I look too long or something?

A bit later I went for a cheeky piss in the beach bar. He was standing by the little ice-cream kiosk thing. He pulled down his Ray-Bans an inch to look me in the eye. *Faggot*, I thought, and scowled at him. But when I came out of the lavs, he'd moved down the path towards the sand dunes you have to walk through to get to the beach. They were covered with shrubs and trees, winding up into the hillside away from the beach.

Fernando made sure I'd seen him and then vanished off the path and into the trees. My heart was all the way up in my throat. I was more awake than I'd ever, ever been. I knew what he was up to. My head was telling me to go back to my towel, but my feet – and my schlong, if I'm honest – told me to follow him. And so I did. I literally strayed from the path and followed him into the sand dunes, my Havaianas filling with sand every step of the way.

He was tucked away in a little clearing between some trees. *He's probably a murderer,* a little voice kept saying, but I swear I could feel adrenaline pounding through my body.

We never said a word. He just yanked my board shorts down and got on with it.

When it was all over, and Fernando walked away without a goodbye, everything felt very real. It didn't feel like porn any more, it felt grainy and shit. I puked in the sand. I went back to the lads and said I had a headache. I had to get in the shower and get him off me.

The funny thing is, although I knew I shouldn't have done it and it scared the crap out of me, every time I thought about it, for months after, I got a lob on. I watched a bit of bi porn and stuff. You know what? Sooner or later I think I knew I'd need that high again.

Bing bong. The train announcer says we're pulling into York station. Shit. That means we've only got Darlington and Newcastle to go. My mouth is dry as Ghandi's flip-flop. I feel rank. Is it peppermint tea that's meant to be good for your stomach? I text Ade to ask. He knows about tea and stuff like that. He can make food that's not from frozen. Maybe I'll get a cup of that.

Me and Ellie were totally mature and grown-up like and decided to call it a day before we went away. It was sad as fuck. She was going to St Andrews and I'm at Liverpool, so it was never gonna work. We both knew. What's funny is that when we were applying for universities, us going to the same place was never on the table.

The thing with Ellie and me is that we were best friends. When I was with her I didn't have to be Hunky Dunc and she didn't have to be Little Miss Perfect.

We could just *be*. Sometimes it felt like we had an arrangement. Does that make sense?

When I emailed her and told her I was seeing a fella, I was scared shitless, but she just said she was thrilled for me and would I like her to come down to meet him. She gave us her blessing. You know what? I wonder if she knew. I never confessed to her about Fernando, but I wonder if she knew.

I was never planning on ending up with a guy, but that's Ade in a nutshell. I don't think he was gonna take no for an answer.

Halloween. It happened like this: So when I first got here, I joined the hockey team because I was a bit bored of football, to be honest. What I didn't know was that, every year, the hockey team do a naked calendar to raise money for a charity that's trying to stop homophobic bullying. It was too late for me to be in this year's calendar, but there was a Halloween party to launch it, organized with the LGBT Society.

The difference between school and university is that no one here gives a single fuck. Like why *wouldn't* the hockey team and the LGBT society have a party together? It was fancy dress and, with the calendar, a bit of flesh was heartily encouraged. I wore some red Calvins, painted myself red all over and stuck some horns on my head. We looked boss striding through Liverpool pretty much in the buff.

The party was in one of the SU bars. It's a bit of a fleapit, but the music was good and it was £1.50 for a spirit and dash. Get in. Luckily, I didn't have a lecture until eleven the next day so I could get nicely battered.

I clocked the DJ while I was queuing at the bar. He had his top off and was sprayed with gold glitter all over. (Apparently he was Rocky from *Rocky Horror Show*, but I didn't know what that was.) I mostly saw his smile. I know that's a dead mushy thing to say, but when our eyes met, he looked me up and down and just did this giant beaming grin. The UV lights made his teeth glow. He had dimples.

It's a good job I was devil red, because I must have blushed like a proper twat.

Later in the night – several bevvies in – I bumped into him when I was coming out of the lav. I don't know why I'm always meeting guys near toilets. Sketchy. Anyway, he gave us the nod and I nodded back, just to be friendly like. Then he grabbed my arm.

"Hey, are you a fresher?"

"Aye," I said.

"Geordie accent! Love it!" He's from Sarf Landan, innit. "You in the calendar?"

"No, mate."

"Oh, are you here with the Gays?"

"NO!" I held my hands up.

"Calm down, mate. Jesus! Fragile masculinity." The big smile never left his face. His eyes are a lovely warm brown, like Nutella on toast. "I wasn't implying anything. I'm Ade. I *am* with the Gays."

"Sorry. I didn't mean to be such a bag of dicks…"

"Let me guess? Some of your best friends are gay?"

I shook my head, embarrassed. "Not really. I just… My name's Duncan."

We shook hands and it was a bit weird. His hand was firm and warm.

"Well, Duncan, I certainly hope you'll be in next year's calendar. Masturbation material for a whole month."

I laughed. I chanced a look at the bulge in his gold Kylie hotpants. "You not into hockey?"

"Do I fucking look like I play hockey?"

I shrugged. "You … you've got the body for it."

"I work out, innit?" He flexed his arm. They were … good arms. "I don't like hockey, but I do support the hockey team however I can." His smile got even bigger. "And I'm good with secrets." And then he ducked into the loo.

Well, I got wankered and waited for him at the end of the night. "Can we go somewhere for a drink?" I said.

"It's two in the morning!" he said, getting his jacket from the cloakroom. "Where we gonna go?"

"Dunno," I said. P.S. a lot of this is what Ade has *told* me I said – I was obliterated by that point. "Have you got anything to drink at yours?"

He shrugged. "I think there's a bottle of vodka in the freezer. Don't know if I've got anything to mix it with. Milk? Can you mix vodka and milk?"

"I have done and it's rank," I told him.

"Haven't you had enough, mate?"

I shook my head. "We don't even have to drink…"

He rolled his eyes. "Oh, come on, then. Get your coat."

"I didn't bring one, like. I'm from up north – this isn't cold."

He laughed and we walked (staggered) back to

his place. I kept looking over my shoulder, making sure none of the hockey lads saw us leave together. I remember, even through the vodka glaze, being terrified. He put Lana Del Rey on and I perched on the very edge of the bed.

"Maybe I should go," I said, suddenly panicking.

He leaned down. When he kissed me, my whole body shivered, even though his heating was on full. I didn't want to go. All I wanted to do was touch him, touch him everywhere and let my hands go mad, but I knew what that meant.

I knew what *wanting* to do that meant.

But I couldn't not. He looked so good, and he was red hot and he was right there on top of me.

I was pissed. He showed me what to do and I liked it.

When the sun came up, the sheets were covered in body paint and glitter. It looked like a massacre. We were all tangled up together – clammy, salty and naked.

The weirdest thing of all was that I didn't care. I just wanted us to be attached – my chest pressed to his back. I kept waiting for the freakout to happen, but it never came. He even asked.

"Morning," he said, rolling over. "This is the part

where you tell me that if I say anything, you'll kill me."

"Did someone really say that to you?"

"Maybe I'm paraphrasing a little."

I rubbed my face. I felt like twice-microwaved shite. "Fuck, I'm hanging, man. But I thought what we did was mint."

He laughed. "Aye, it was." He did the worst Geordie accent ever.

"If you do *that* again I might kill you like," I said. "Have you got lectures?"

"I study English. I *never* have lectures."

"Awesome. Can I stay here for a bit?"

"Yeah. Do you get the horn when you're hungover?"

"Aye."

It sort of feels like I never left his room after that night. That bed has become our whole world. It was never the plan to meet someone during Fresher's month, but I did. I've made some mates – the psychology lot are wicked – and I'm still playing hockey with the lads, but I spend most of my time with Ade. He's a second year, so he had his mates sorted.

The *other* thing about university was that no one knew Hunky Dunc or Ellie. I never 'came out' because I didn't need to. I couldn't have kept my grubby mitts off Ade even if I'd wanted to and so people just assumed I was gay and always had been. Which is pretty accurate now I think about it. Some of the hockey lads were all like, "Oh, I didn't know you were gay", but they didn't start hiding their todgers in the showers or anything like. They're top lads. Like I said, not a single fuck given.

Except now I do need to come out and I'm bricking it.

See it's always been just Mam and me. Dad jogged on when I was a baby and she never remarried or had any other kids. She's proud of me. She's always saying to her friends, "Ooh, I'm so made up with our Duncan, first one in the family to go off to university! Not a dummy like his mam and dad, is he?" She loved Ellie, too. She didn't talk to us for about a week when I told her we was ending it.

You hear though. You hear stories about gay kids who have to live on the streets and end up as rent boys and stuff. Like would she really throw me out? There's a lesbian in the office she works at and when she married her partner, Mum always used speech marks around 'married' and 'wife'. She said it was 'a waste' when Tom Daley came out.

OK, I don't think she's gonna come at me with a knife or anything, but everything between me and Mam is priceless and perfect, like a Ming vase or something, and I'm about to smash it all to shit and be like, "Put that back together, then". Nothing's ever gonna be the same again.

I'm about to kill everything we've got, and what I suppose it boils down to is… What if she doesn't love me any more? That'd be shit.

But then I think about Ade again and let all his light wash through me. Last week we went ice-skating – they've set up a temporary rink outside the museum. To say I'm pretty nifty on my feet on the pitch, I was freaking hopeless on ice. My knees were folding in and I had to cling to the side like a limpet while actual infants zoomed past me. Of course Ade was like fucking Torvill AND Dean, making me look even worse. "Come on, you dick, just hold my hand. I've got you."

He took my hand in one of his mittens. I was terrified I'd go down and one of the bastard kids would slice my fingers off. "Just lock your knees. I've got you."

We cautiously skated out away from the boundary. Clinging to Ade, I was able to find my feet.

"I look like a proper wanker," I said.

"No one in the whole wide world has ever looked as beautiful as you do in this precise moment."

I laughed and almost fell flat on my arse. He caught me and we went down together.

*

Mam is waiting for me in the car park at Newcastle station. It's dark by the time the train rolls in. Sorry to be a cliché, but I really have brought a mountain of laundry in a big wheelie case. Mam sees me coming in the rear-view mirror and pops the boot.

"Hiya, pet," she says. "How was the trip up?" She's had her hair cut a little bit shorter and it's blonder than when I went away.

"Yeah, it was fine," I say. I feel sick.

Now is not the time.

"Don't fanny about, I've got dinner on a low heat."

I climb into the passenger seat. Local radio is playing. Her stilettos lie in the footwell of the passenger side because she can't drive in heels.

"What are we having?" I ask.

"Cottage pie and beans," she says. "When was the

last time you had a proper meal, eh?"

Last night. Ade cooked lamb massaman curry as a goodbye dinner. I could tell her that. I could just say, "My boyfriend cooks for me all the time".

No. Now is not the time.

"I dunno," I say as she pulls out of the car park.

"I hope you're not just eating kebabs and junk."

"I can't afford kebabs," I tell her. "It's pasta and sauce most nights." That's another thing – I rely on my allowance from Mam. Sure, I've got my loan, but she sends two hundred quid a month and I really need it. What if she cuts me off?

We live in Jesmond, a little drive outside of the city centre. She turns into our cul-de-sac and the familiarity feels warm. I've lived on this street my whole life – same semi-detached house. I've missed home this term, not full-on homesickness, but home is ... home. This is where I'm from.

As ever, the heating is on full-blast as we step inside and the house is thick with rich, meaty cottage pie smell. My mouth waters. The cat, an unimpressed little knobhead at the best of times, gives me the shit-eye – peering down at me through the stair rails.

"I'll stick a load on after dinner, just leave your case in the hall. Go wash your hands and I'll get dinner on the plate."

I wonder if she's missed having someone to fuss over. I wash my hands in the downstairs loo before kicking off my trainers and padding through to the dining room. I'd forgotten what proper carpet feels like on your feet: lovely and squishy.

"Do you like my new wallpaper?" she calls from the kitchen.

She's been excited about showing me the new dining room. "Aye, it's mint," I call back. It's a bit flowery for me, but she seems dead keen. Hands wrapped in cherry-red oven gloves, she carries two steaming plates through. Mam believes serving food on cold plates should be a criminal offence.

She plonks a plate in front of me. "Do you want any sauce or anything?"

"No, thanks."

"There's more Bisto in the pan if you want it."

"Cool." I tuck in.

"So how's your lectures going, pet?"

"Aye, not bad."

164

"Do you still think you'll change courses?"

"Maybe. This is really nice, Mam." Now that I'm here, it feels like I'm in a world without Ade, a world where I'm ten years old again. I can't imagine telling her about my boyfriend because that person – that version of me – doesn't live here.

There's a little silence. Mam puts more salt on her cottage pie.

I can't do it. The lights on the Christmas tree change colour every five seconds and I can't ruin Christmas. Maybe I'll wait until next week.

"Listen, son. I want to talk about this gay thing."

I swear my heart actually stops. For a second I'm legally dead. My throat closes up. "What?" I rasp.

Her mouth is a tight line. "I can't have it hanging over me all Christmas," she says. "I won't be able to have any fun at all, so let's just get it out of the way now."

"I don't know what you mean," I lie.

"I wasn't born yesterday, Duncan. There I am typing 'Gardening Centre' into Google when 'Gaytube' and 'Gaydar' pop up, and it wasn't me that went on those websites and it wasn't the ruddy cat either, was it?"

Fuck. How? I always clear my history. I only went on

those sites out of nosiness anyways, like.

Shit.

Apparently now *is* the time.

I can't speak. I just stare at my cottage pie.

"I'm not cross, you know," she says, her voice tiny. "I still love yous."

I can't look at her. "I was going to tell you," I mutter.

"I didn't want to believe it, but then I spoke to your auntie Julie and she talked some sense into me. She said, 'He's still your Duncan, isn't he?' and I was like, 'Aye, I suppose he is'. I just want yous to be happy, Duncan."

A tear rolls down my cheek and plops into my tea. "I am happy."

"Have you got a fella, then?"

I nod.

"What's he like?"

"I love him."

"Does he love you?"

"Aye."

"And he treats you right?"

"Aye."

"Good. What's his name?"

"Ade. He's a top lad."

She sighs deeply. "I won't lie, Duncan, it's all a lot to take in. I worry about you, pet."

I finally look up. "You don't have to worry about me. He's awesome."

"Well, like I say, if you're happy, I'm happy. And I mean that." She goes to the kitchen and fetches the kitchen roll. "Here – there's no need to cry."

I wipe my eyes. I feel lighter somehow. "I was so worried about coming home. I didn't know what you were gonna say. I've been proper stressing about it, like."

She shakes her head. "Did you really think I'd kick off? You and me aren't going anywhere, are we? There's nothing you could say to me that'd make me love you less – you should know that. Except voting for the bastard Tories," she says, with a wink.

I laugh and she smiles back at me. She takes my hand and gives it a squeeze. "So tell me all about this Ade character, then."

And look at that, the world is still turning.

Amir and George

*

Sita Brahmachari

Road is moving too fast.

Mr Shaw he drive high speed to Speech Day final school.

Far I go from Kabir and Mirsa, from petrol smell of city, out from shadows of tower blocks. Only fields are here. More birds, no people. It is too quiet. Looks like Mr Shaw and me have moved to new land.

Look out of the window, Amir, I say myself. Look out!

Where there is houses in village, windows show Christmas tree lights shining and I feel little better. But everything I am watching from outside. Like last week in class we watch 'Christmas Carol' by Charles Dickens, when this boy is looking at happiness through the window. This is my first Christmas here. I still feeling on outside of window looking in. But I am not tiny boy, like this Tim. People think I am tall and strong-looking, like man. Kabir says to me, "Stop growing, Amir. Your head is already more high over mine!" My father was tall man, not like Kabir.

Mr Shaw is feeling in festival spirit. He sings with radio some words: "Weather outside is frightful…" But he smiles at same time, relaxing in driving.

"Why it is frightening?" I ask.

"*Is it.*" Mr Shaw can't understand how I get so good in English and then I make this simple mistake.

"Why is it frightening?"

"What's frightening?"

"The weather … in song."

"No, not frightening, Amir… *Frightful*… It means bad weather!"

"So why are they happy to be with bad weather?"

Mr Shaw laughs. "The lyric's about feeling warm and comfortable in your house while the weather is cold outside."

It is warm in the car, but I am cold. Now I am thinking it is my fault how I come in this situation. I am for blame alone. I see this question for public-speaking competition outside Mr Shaw's office. I sign my name on list. I say to my friend Mo, "You enter with me." But he say, "This is not for us. They will make fools from us." Now I wish I listen to him.

"Have you been out of the city before?" Mr Shaw asks me.

"No, never."

"You've come a long way, Amir, in just one year!"

I think long, long way and this is long, long road.

"What do you make of the countryside?"

"I don't know it."

"I'm a country boy myself. You can take the country out of the boy, Amir, but you can't take the boy out of the country."

"This is true! You will never take my country out from me," I tell Mr Shaw.

He looks at me then back to motorway. "I'm sure that's right, Amir."

Mr Shaw is looking like he's young man, not wearing his worrying lines across forehead like he wears in school. But I am opposite. My heart is not light, not comfortable. It fires in my chest like shelling.

"Mr Shaw, I change my idea. I cannot give Public Speech at final."

Mr Shaw stops the radio. "But Amir… *You* persuaded *me* that you should do it. I wasn't sure, but you've proved me wrong. You've done so well to get this far. Don't give up now. Anyway, you've given that speech so many times – you know it off by heart."

"Yes, confidence is OK in the city … not in this country."

"But Amir, this is the same country. It's just the country*side*, that's all."

"For you maybe so. You feel more in home here, I feel better in city."

My mind runs slow with many new pictures after we drive from the city. Too many new pictures, too much thinking – like computer when many windows are keep open. Memory is full. I am in fear I will forget my speech, forget how to speak in English. Strength in mind is leaking from me.

*

We leave motorway road and now car is driving on long road with sheep on one side, sheep on other. Very slowly car is judder-judder over metal.

"Bloody cattle grids!" Mr Shaw is swearing. "Sorry,

excuse my language! The school's not far now, should be just around the corner."

Now my mouth is open like eating air. Speech Final school is in front like grey castle.

We walk on stone path. Not so long past, I walked from forest on path like this, with broken shoes.

"Shiny shoes, Amir!"

"Kabir polished them ready and Mirsa bought this new shirt. She says old school shirt is looking grey not white. I don't know."

"They did well. You look smart!"

"They are wanting to come here today. For supporting me. I told Kabir it is not permitted. So he tells me – Amir, I will shine these shoes. Then, when you look on them, you must think Kabir's confidence thoughts."

Reception is big hall with tall stairs winding round and round. I look up to the top at paintings with gold frames showing people with expression to painter saying, "I am very important person – V.I.P." Giant faces staring on me from paintings. One woman with closed tight lips and white hair, wearing blue coat. I can hear this lady's sharp voice in my head – says,

"Go home, Amir Karoon. You do not belong here."

Steps are wide and made in wood, not like concrete stairs of my school. In this landing here is painting of tall man wearing same blue coat. I ask Mr Shaw why all wear same blue dress coat and flat black cap.

"Graduation gowns and mortar boards," he explains. "You'll wear one of those one day, Amir – when you finish university!"

I don't know.

At top of stairs there is other painting. This man is not wearing gown and black hat. He is different looking. Black hair, moustache … not so sharp. He is looking little piece like my father, how I remember him. Expression like his eyes are holding burning questions.

"The man himself – George Orwell – the reason we're here! Come on, Amir. Let's do this thing."

Mr Shaw's arm is round my shoulder, walking me inside this hall.

So many hundreds students. Voices echo up to top seats, like screech of seabirds.

There is one Christmas tree with sparkle lights, this is most giant inside tree I ever seen.

"What a tree! You can smell the needles in the air."

Often Mr Shaw he tells things I don't know what it means, but I don't ask every time. It makes me feel like small child knowing nothing. Needles in the air?

"Smell this pine, Amir!" Mr Shaw he takes some green spike from the tree, squeezes juice in fingers and gives to me. I test how sharp.

"Smells fresh, like sleeping in forest," I tell him.

Then he looks to me, like he sometimes looks to me. Not funny now, like he is worrying.

Hall is coming quiet. Announcer Lady with hair in tight knot and black suit comes in stage. She says welcome to finals of George Orwell National Writing and Public Speaking Competition. She says we are all winning. I don't know why she says this. If so, why is it competition? Why do we come here? She asks all Final people to walk to stage and sit in seats. I stand like robot. I hear Mr Shaw say, "I'm proud of you, Amir Karoon."

I don't want him to think I chicken so I walk to the front. I have no thoughts in mind. I have walk like this before – when I did not know which direction I will turn.

Announcer Lady gives me number card. I am seven. There are ten finalists, always ten. In past I like this number ten – not any more. The girl in front of me, number six, she looks like Mikah how she would grow ... *if* she would grow.

Now Announcer Lady is saying we are lucky to have important judges. She says announcement of names and each panel person stands and students is clapping. There is writer, politician, history professor and actor. When Actor Lady stands ... I think I have seen in TV, but I don't know. She smiles, bows and all the people in this hall cheer and clap, stamping feet.

Announcer Lady welcomes first speaker to stage to address question for George Orwell competition: "If Liberty means anything at all, it means the right to tell people what they do not want to hear."

Number one is standing. Shoulders are wide. Even more wide from mine. His voice is like posh person. If you take film and say this boy is Prime Minister in five years' time, I believe you. He is saying about what is means by 'equality in society'. His speech is smooth, clear, easy. Then next speaker comes. Thing in every speech is strong statistics, numbers, repeating phrase to make point. I don't know half of words. There is much I cannot understand. Number four boy is using all good technique, speaking in confidence, but his eyes stay like ice.

Now it is girl next to me. She is talking of racism. This I understand, but she takes different direction. She is giving interesting facts of racism in wide society, things she is saying I have not been thinking about before … like asking why so little diversity people are going to university. She is saying also about young black men in prison and how many cannot read. I did not know this. It is strange in such rich country, people cannot read. I really did not know these things. Now she is telling of gangs and why should people want to join. What is motivation? She is even doing some rap music, getting people to rap and clap with her. She is not copying format how to speak. She is someone who has her heart on fire.

I look to Mr Shaw. I shake my head like to say warning, "I can't do this". He only smiles at me. My speech is like different species. My speech is only my story. Number six girl is finishing now and every person is clapping. Actor Lady is standing and cheering. I think this girl must be winning. I hope she is.

"Thank you, Grace!" Announcer Lady tries to make people stop clapping. They don't want to. Now she must shout over clapping, using her hands to make audience quiet.

Number six girl called Grace tells, "Your turn". I don't know why I think her eyes are looking so like Mikah.

"Amir Karoon." Announcer Lady is calling my name. "Amir Karoon."

Looking at my shoes, my legs are shaking. Now I am happy Kabir is not here to see me fail. My friend Mo will think I am fool. He will say, "Yes, I told you it will be shame for us this way."

"Amir Karoon."

Grace is saying to me, "That's you, isn't it?"

I want to say Grace, *I don't know what is me in this place.*

I stand. I have no notes like others. But I like to try to get things right, perfect like I can, so I learn this speech in heart … *by* heart. So my speech is better than the way I speak English. I speak like a script I learn of my story, mistakes taken out … most of time.

In trials people like my speech, even if English is not perfect. People are voting to support me … maybe not only me, but also feeling about refugee children. I am representing. I do this not only for me. This I tell myself, trying to build some confidence.

I am looking for place in hall to focus. I choose the star at high point of Christmas tree and I start to speak. But my voice is weak. Mr Shaw is smiling too much. Christmas light is shining on my eyes. I am thinking where is this tree come from? Maybe even the forest I hide in.

Each speech I start in same way. I remember the words I write in my heart and I start to speak. Mr Shaw tells me, "Imagine words like a river flowing."

I am Amir Karoon. This is my story. I have lived in this country for one year. This is my first competition I take part in representing my school. When I heard of George Orwell competition, I went to my teacher Mr Shaw and I observe to him … my English is not so good, but I can tell you something about this subject: 'If Liberty means anything at all, it means the right to tell people what they do not want to hear'.

I am speaking, but audience is looking one to other

like something is wrong. Actor Lady is looking down at table, shaking head like she will cry. People move around in seats, whispering.

Mr Shaw is standing, making others move in row, excuse me, excuse me. Walking through hall. Now he is taking me by shoulder.

Announcer Lady is saying, "There will be a short interval. Please remain seated – we will recommence in a few minutes."

People starting talking. I can hear in their voices they pay me pity. I am sad loser boy they will go home and talk... I am foreign boy they will say ... he is nothing, should not be making speech with so little English.

Mr Shaw takes me to room with one mirror, chair and soft sofa seat. He says it is a dressing room for theatre performance. I don't care what is.

Mr Shaw is wearing deep lines. "What happened, Amir?"

"I was telling my speech like all the other times."

Mr Shaw is shaking his head. "Amir, I'm so sorry. You froze when you stood up there. I should have gone with my instinct. I should never have put you through this."

"I know these words by my heart! I want to smash my stupid head."

"Don't be so hard on yourself, Amir. You won't be the first or the last to get stage fright! Let me go and speak to the judges and see what happens now." He is biting lips like he is not sure what to do.

Mr Shaw opens the door wide. I hear clapping. "They must have started again... Amir, I'll be back in a minute."

Words are in my head like waves moving in and out... Frightful, stage fright, frightening, fear, fear... Fear made me silent Boy again, made me suck on bitter lemon-half. I am looking at my face in a mirror. Lights on border make my grey eyes shine.

My eyes grow bigger. In reflection I see other face. Behind in chair is sitting tall man, black hair, small glasses, wool jacket, moustache. Question in eyes. He smiles at me.

I don't know to turn or no, so I stay looking in the mirror.

"You're George Orwell, from the painting in hall?" I say to reflection.

"I am. And who are you?"

"Amir Karoon."

"So tell me, Amir Karoon. What did you come here to say?"

"You looking little like my father," I tell him. I begin to turn to talk with him.

"Amir, don't turn around. Please let me hear your story." Reflection George takes a book from his pocket and a pen.

"What are you writing in your book?"

"Meeting with Amir Karoon... Old habits!" He smiles at me. I don't get this, but I feel in my heart he is a good man like Kabir, like Mr Shaw. "Take your time."

I sit tall and take deep breaths. Then I look him in his reflection face.

*

I am Amir Karoon. This is my story. When I heard of George Orwell competition, I went to my teacher Mr Shaw and I observe to him ... my English is not so good, but I can tell you something about this subject: "If Liberty means anything at all, it means the right to tell people what they do not want to hear."

*

"I like that title," George reflection says, leans forward in his chair. "Go on!"

*

This is not the country I am born in. My land is Iraq. I came here one year ago, when I was thirteen years old. Now I am fourteen. When I come ... came here, I had little English. When I came here I had not much speech at all. My speaking voice I think was buried in war ... ash and dirt. You see I was looking for my mother, my father, my brother Suli, under fallen wall of my garden. I find ... I found nothing but one lemon. I put it in my pocket. I think how it is ... how is it—"

*

"Don't worry! It is, is it – just speak, Amir!" Reflection George says.

*

How is it possible I can find this lemon and not my parents? Days I look for them. I am hungry. I am thirsty. Bitter taste is in my mouth, like in my heart.

I look down on my feet and they are walking.

Like they know better than me, I must leave to survive. In my mouth I hold the lemon-half. My face is swollen like fish shape. I suck in bitter taste, I walk, I cry, I taste the bitter, I walk, I cry. I follow others. I do not know where we go, but it is somewhere. Only one thing I know is we walk away from my home, my land.

Sometime people talk to me at border ... at checkpoint. I have no papers.

One soldier he ask me, "Where do you go?"

I stay silent.

He asks me, "How old you are?"

I do not answer.

Then he pays me pity. "Go through, go through, son. Try to join another family. You must walk three days to get to camp for refugees. Inshallah you are strong boy, you will be safe."

I think maybe camp can be a better place for me.

This is the moment I must step away and be Boy. If I stay Amir, I cannot speak this part of the story. This is the moment I ask you to switch off pictures you see on news, step sideways out of your everyday mind, like when doors slide from real world into dreams.

Boy is walking.

*

"And that boy is you. Isn't it, Amir?" Reflection George says.

I nod. I turn to see if he is real.

"Don't turn back now, Amir… Go on!" he says.

*

Boy is walking. A strange boy who sucks a lemon in his mouth.

What is he walking away from?

Death.

What is he walking towards?

Life.

Boy will ask each one of you if you will do the same in his shoes. He thinks you will.

Boy is in search of a sweet taste. He can tell you this. If you eat too much poison it takes long, long time to feel sweet again.

Camp is not the home Boy hopes for. Camp is many people. Many, many people who want only to be home. Camp is a dangerous place for this silent boy.

Boy sees many things. Many people here have

poison flowing in their blood. Poison makes them ill, like good meat when flies suck too long in heat.

One night into his tent walks a man of rock. Boy calls him Rock Heart.

He says Boy must go with him. He says he takes children to freedom. He says, "You must not speak. You must be silent."

He does not know Boy has lemon-half in mouth. Only if he spits it, he can speak and Boy has no wish to speak. Rock Heart takes Boy's hands and pulls him out of tent. Boy starts new life, but this man does not care to give Boy a name.

In that night, in that darkness, Rock Heart takes five boys, five girls from camp. On many days walking, Rock Heart is not kind. He is not gentle. He is not good. Boy does not like the way he looks at girls, especially Mikah from Boy's village. Rock Heart has wanting eyes like grown man should not look to young girl. Boy holds Mikah's hand to keep her safe. Rock Heart man spits on Boy. "What are you, fish face! Her great protector?"

"Hurry, hurry," he say. "We must reach the sea for dawn breaking."

Boy is afraid of sea. He cannot swim.

Rock Heart pushes Boy inside the boat. Boat is not good looking. Boat is soft like toy you take for holiday.

"Look after this lot! Valuable cargo if you can get them to the other side," Rock Heart tells Cargo Man. Boy sees they are passing money one to other. Cargo Man touches Mikah's hair. Making of her beauty a joke. She is starting to cry. Boy knows no one cares for them – all the children know this. Only Cargo Man is wearing jacket for saving his life.

Boy makes decision. If he gets to land in safety, he will run from Cargo Man. He will take Mikah with him somewhere no one may find them. Boy knows Cargo Man does not think to make them free. Poison blood … corruption like disease is spreading.

Sea is quiet in first hours. Moon is like a silver coin. Sea and sky are no difference – where one ends, other begins. Only land is missing. Stars is our universe shining. Boy wishes on light of universe to take him to safe place, Inshallah.

Boy is on the boat
Sun rise, slow, pink, orange

Red scar dawn
Stomach heaves into Boy's mouth
Sick is in the boat
Stink is bitter
Boy sucks on bitter. It is nothing new
Best time of day is the time of two lights
Twilight
Where moon and sun kiss
Then the sky is full of magic colours
Anything can happen
In his mind Boy sings to Mikah every night they live
 on boat
Sea stays calm for one whole night, then comes the
 anger storm
Boy is sure all must die
Sun sets like giant blood-red eye.

*

Cargo Man's eyes are full from fear. He shouts for children to still. He stands. But children don't stop screaming. Maybe sea hears them cry. Wave rises up like justice hand from bottom of sea, reaches into boat and takes only Cargo Man.

Children are silent, holding for life on to rings on side of boat. Children are all hating Cargo Man ... but now he is not here to hate.

Boy lies on the floor of boat. Sea is calm but sun is cooking skin. Lips are dry. Mikah sleeps on Boy's knee. Boy watches the waves. Mikah's head is a ball of fire. She is the sun.

Boy falls deep in sleep. In his dream Boy reaches land, takes Mikah's hand and runs away.

It is twilight, but now the sun is leaving fast. Boy takes lemon-half from mouth, kisses Mikah's head and holds and holds her. She is cold, but still he holds her. How many days must they rock like this together? Dead girl, living boy. Boy sleeps, he wakes, he sleeps, he wakes. There is no water, no more dreams of happiness. Boy closes eyes and prays to Allah for what is his will. He sleeps again and when he wakes there is land in the distance... Rescue boat comes to find ... one boat with ten children. Only three are living.

Boy will not let Mikah go. Rescue people pull her from him and he screams like a wolf in the night. Then he puts the lemon in his mouth and sucks.

They take Boy to another kind of camp — with high wire walls. But before the wire, Boy escapes and runs and runs and runs into the forest. He lies on earth floor, face in dirt, and cries. He hears others in the wood. He is thinking, I am dreaming. He does not know how long he stays like this.

A woman's hands are on his shoulders turning him, speaking in his tongue. "Is that you, Amir? Are you alone?"

This woman speaks Boy's name. It is Mirsa from Boy's village and Kabir. Friends of his parents. Mirsa takes the lemon from his mouth and gives him water.

They have baby Kalila ... a daughter maybe six months old, but they hold Boy like he is their own son. They cry to hear Boy's story. They sing and pray for all the leaving and the lost. They eat what they find in the wood — berries and mushrooms. Slowly, slowly, Boy starts to hear his name. Slowly, slowly, he becomes Amir again.

*

Kabir has a plan. They say they have family in England and I should go with them. There are people who will come to help, but until this time, everywhere we go we must hide. We must not be seen.

Happy times and hungry times were in the forests. Mirsa singing to baby Kalila and me singing, too. After song one day, Mirsa tells me that if we go to England she will make me like her son. Then she will have one son, one daughter.

I keep the lemon in my pocket.

After the forest I take fever in my head. I cannot remember all this journey. Mirsa says it is good to not remember everything. It is mercy.

My body aches like I am bruise from monster lorry journey. We are like chickens packed inside on way to new camp they call jungle.

A jungle is beautiful in my mind
A jungle is green with lions and tigers, elephants and
   monkeys, bright birds
A jungle smells of heat … coconut oil, eucalyptus
This is not a jungle
This is like people growing from mud and human
   waste
Shit.

*

They say they will come to jungle and destroy the school, our mosque, the church, the fields of tents. They will not let us stay here. Kabir tells we will go before that time. We have an arrangement.

One night he wakes and we walk away... "Quiet, quiet, be silent now, Amir."

I hold the lemon in my mouth.

"I said three... The agreement was three," Frozen Man says.

He is Rock Heart and Cargo Man all together – cares only for money.

Mirsa tells him, "Look, the baby is like carrying nothing."

Frozen Man says, "Everything costs money ... 'nothing' could be very costly if it cries."

"I will feed her," Mirsa tells ... but Mirsa has no milk left.

Kabir and Mirsa they pay for me because they know my mother and father, because with everything that has happened to them, they do not let the poison enter in their blood.

Mirsa says to me, "Amir, you will bring us good fortune, Inshallah."

Frozen Man closes the door of giant fridge, slams it, locks it. He tells us to be quiet 'like nothing'. I show him lemon in my mouth. He looks to me like I am idiot boy, but I suck on hate for him.

Sucking lemon harder, gum is bleeding. Blood is freezing. We hold together to stay warm. We hold together for memory of our village.

Mirsa is trying to feed Kalila not to cry
Kalila cries
We are ice breathing
Brain is freezing
Then we are all sleeping
I am not bringing good fortune for Kabir and Mirsa
Kalila stops crying
Kalila cannot wake
Kalila never wakes
She is frozen in death
We are frozen inside and outside.

*

Reflection George is placing his head in hands and shaking, shaking. "I am so sorry, Amir. Even I didn't forsee a world this ugly."

"It is not all ugly," I tell.

*

This is my family now. They finally adopt me and now we are trying to make a place for ourselves in the city.

Mirsa is not my mother
Kabir is not my father
They have no more daughter
I am not their son
This is not my country
But still we are some kind of family together
The lemon from my garden is dried now but I keep it
   to remember.

*

Perhaps my story is not easy for you to hear. Maybe some people do not want to hear, but still I think it is one I must tell because I am alive. This is my liberty.

*

Mr Shaw opens the door. "I'm sorry, Amir. I'm afraid there's not going to be an opportunity for you to speak today. The rules are quite firm. I hope you're not too disappointed. Do you want to stay to see who wins?"

Behind me I see the chair is empty.

Reflection is gone.

We walk out into the hall. I turn to see the painting of George Orwell. I did not notice before, this gentle smile. He is looking like gentle man, like my teacher.

"No, Mr Shaw. I don't care who wins. Let us go home."

The Letter

*

Tracy Darnton

'The Letter' is the winning story from the
Stripes YA Short Story Prize in partnership with
The Bookseller. *Congratulations, Tracy!*

It's hard to imagine, but the Bowling Plaza is even worse than usual tonight. A bobbing, giant inflatable snowman is tethered to the roof, casting menacing shadows over the car park. Inside they've strung up cheap tinsel and 'Season's Greetings' banners, and a plastic tree with red and green baubles sits on the reception desk, getting in the way. It's only the first day of December, but already there's a sickly smell of stale mulled wine and a drunken office party is messing about by the pool tables.

Spotty Paul on shoe duty is dressed as an elf. You'd think he'd have more respect for himself. I don't like doing anything where you have to wear communal shoes. I've had enough of hand-me-down crap. Paul sprays them with a sickly aerosol between each customer, but even so, it freaks me out. I shudder as I put them on. This interests Julie and she makes a note in her stripy book as usual.

"Maybe it's due to my feelings of abandonment," I tell her helpfully so she has something else to write down. "Or maybe it's because I dislike other people's smelly feet – which is completely rational, by the way."

Can you believe Social Services still has a budget for bowling and ice cream with Julie? The free ice cream would be OK if I was, like, six years old and on a beach. I'd rather have a double shot Americano. But I don't want a machine coffee in a plastic cup, so I stare for a while at the ice-cream choices to build the suspense before saying, "Nothing, thanks."

Julie looks disappointed. Maybe because she is now a grown woman licking a Solero next to a teenage girl sipping at a cup of water. I tell Julie she should cut back on the ice creams. If she takes all her clients out like this, no wonder.

"No wonder, Julie," I say, tutting.

Julie reddens and makes another note. Does she ever just call it as it is and write 'Bitch' or does she always have some mumbo-jumbo excuse for my behaviour?

"So who's drawn the short straw this year?" I ask.

"We're having a little trouble getting the right placement for you after term finishes," says Julie, fidgeting. This is Julie-speak for 'nobody wants you'.

"How will Santa know where to find me?" I stare, wide-eyed. I see her processing whether I'm serious or not. She just doesn't get irony. I learned the truth about Father Christmas early on in life.

To be honest, I see the Christmas stuff happening around me like a trailer for a film I don't get to watch in full; like those adverts on TV where one big happy family sits down at a glittering table with a shiny turkey and everybody is so frigging happy. It's not my world. I'm like the Ghost of Christmas No One Wants in a foster home. They have to pretend to like me and cover up the fact their own child gets piles of gifts from relatives who actually give a shit.

"So no room at the inn," I say and laugh. "That reminds me of something."

"It'll be fine." Julie pats my hand. I shrug her off.

"Tell them it's only dogs who aren't just for Christmas – you can get rid of kids, no problem," I say. "Anyway, I don't know what all the fuss is. It's just a day when the shops shut and the telly's better."

Julie's Solero is dripping down her hand. I watch as the drip plops on to her lap.

"Can't I stay at Beechwood by myself?" I already know the answer.

The office party's getting rowdier, singing along to piped Christmas singles from last century. Paul the elf has to intervene.

I start bowling with Julie. "The sooner we begin, the sooner it's over," I say. We take the furthest alley as usual, like an old married couple picking their regular table at the pizzeria.

I watch as she bowls. The ball trickles down the polished lane, heading slowly for the gutter at the side. She looks surprised. I don't know why. She's always rubbish at this. I used to think she was letting me win and hate her for it, as if my winning a game of ten-pin bowling would make everything all right in Julie-land.

She keeps asking me if I'm OK, if I'm having a good time. Please! In this place? She's poking in her bag and casting glances my way like she's got more to tell me. I know the signs.

I win the game, by the way. I always win at things that don't matter.

"I have some news," says Julie, when we stop for her to take a rest and guzzle a fizzy drink.

Finally. What now?

"We've had a letter for you. From your dad. How do you feel about that?" She is obsessed, literally obsessed, with how I feel about everything. "We've struggled to find him, as you know. There was some confusion over names and information." She rummages in her briefcase and hands me an envelope, opened. It sits in my hand like an unexploded bomb.

"If you don't want to look at it today, we can save it for another time. This must all be a big surprise," says Julie. She pats my knee. "Turns out he was back in *America*." She says it like that's an achievement – like he's a film star rather than a waster.

STRIKE! The teenagers on the alley next to us are doing a moonwalk as the scoring machine flashes and plays loud music.

What am I doing in this shitty place?

I look carefully at the envelope addressed to Somerset Social Services. The idiots must have told him where I ended up. I flip it over. The return address is a place in Florida. I can picture it already – a duplex on a housing estate surrounded by retired golfers and repossessions.

Julie checks her watch. Her concern for me only operates until eight o'clock. She has to get back to her real life. She fiddles with the wedding ring on her pudgy hand.

I breathe. I listen to the clatter of the bowling lanes and the whoops of another strike.

"OK," I say. "I'll read it." I remove the letter from the envelope with my fingertips as if it's hot. It's oh-so-carefully typed, but I'm not fooled by him – unlike Julie and her team.

F.A.O. Amber Fitzpatrick

Dear Amber,

I can't tell you how pleased I was to finally have news of you. It was like Jesus himself had answered my prayers. I'm sorry for your loss. I can only imagine what you've been through. But you don't need to worry about anything now – I'm here for you.

Your mom made it pretty difficult after we split up, but I never stopped looking for the pair of you. You know I'd never give up. I went to your old addresses, but you'd moved on every time. You always were a hard girl to pin down, Amber. I can't wait to see what a beautiful young woman you've grown into.

I look forward to rekindling that special bond between us.

Your loving father

"Short but sweet," says Julie. "He's been looking for you all this time."

There's nothing *sweet* about the bastard, but then she's never met him. She knows nothing real about him. About him and me. I promised Mum in one of her lucid episodes that I'd never tell anyone what he used to do to her ... to me. He damaged her forever as sure as if he'd poured the alcohol and the pills down her throat himself. Some secrets are safer kept – especially when your dad's not the forgiving type.

It dawns on me that Julie's probably thinking Dad's the Christmas miracle, appearing to solve all her problems with placing me. She's seeing a happy reunion in Disney World. But that's the last thing I want. And now he's found me, I know there's no way Julie can keep me safe. Not from him. And I can't rely on anybody but me.

"So how do you feel about your dad getting back in touch?"

Feelings again. Always feelings.

She checks her notebook. "It's been a while since you've seen him. We had a lucky break in tracking him down at last."

Lucky? He always was a lucky bastard. After all Mum's efforts with fake names and addresses to make sure the do-gooders couldn't find him, even when she was in rehab and I was playing foster-care roulette.

"Would you like to write back?"

"No need," I say.

"You may feel that now," starts Julie, "but let's talk about it again when you've thought about it some more, maybe chat it through with Dr Meadows. It's a lot to take in, sweetie."

And as usual she's got the wrong end of the stick. She hasn't actually read the letter properly. She doesn't know how my father operates – but I do. Ten days have passed since the postage date. He'll be on his way

– if he's not already here. I look around me, suspicious now of the office partygoers. I need to make plans. I have to disappear.

"Now that your mum is…" Julie pulls awkwardly at her necklace.

"Dead, you mean."

"…No longer here, we could explore other family options."

Family? My dad? I'd rather be shacked up with some cardboard and a blanket in the multi-storey car park. Mum and I did it to get away from him before. All I have to do is keep moving, making it harder for him to find me again. And yet now … now I have more to lose. I have what Julie would call prospects. My grades are good, I wanted to go to university. I have actual friends and decent teachers. Not that I'd ever tell them that.

Julie puffs to her feet and waddles over to choose a bowling ball. "Come on, double or quits."

I think of my neat little room at Beechwood: the duvet cover that Julie and I picked out at Primark, the posters I carefully stuck to the wall and the row of books on the shelf. There's a bright orange cushion

Julie bought me for my birthday that I pretended not to like. Too big to pack now. The furniture is brown and slightly tatty, circa 1999, but everyone's room is like that. I don't stand out among the boarders – except in the holidays.

Julie heads off to the ladies after all that Diet Coke, while I stare at the wall and try to think straight. I thought I'd made myself invisible, but then Julie's boss ruins it all by interfering in my business. The letter has tracked me down like a heat-seeking missile and I'm not free of him even at the shitty Bowling Plaza. I dig my fingernails into the palm of my hand, cross with myself for getting complacent, for getting to like somewhere, when I should have known it wouldn't last.

*

Julie hugs me in the car once we've pulled up outside Beechwood. I let her. She won't be seeing me again. I bite my lip and stare out at the flickering lights on the tree by the main entrance. The angel at the top has broken and the wings are blinking on and off. I was going to help decorate the hall with holly and ivy next week. Proper greenery from the garden – real decorations, not ones made of foil and plastic.

"It feels like snow's on the way," says Julie. "A white Christmas maybe."

A cold one, then. Shit.

"Could I have some extra cash?" I ask. "I need some toiletries and stuff."

She marks it in her notebook and hands me £30.

"I'll see you next week. We can write a response to your dad's letter together, if you like. No pressure. Whatever's best for you." She smiles. "Maybe with Christmas coming…"

She's happier being useful, making plans.

"Sure. I'll think about it." I shove the cash in my pocket and toss her a bone: "I know I can be a right cow sometimes."

She blushes, unsure what to say to that as it's so true. I can't help but feel slightly fond of her and her flowery smocks.

"Take care of yourself," she says.

I intend to.

"We'll sort something out for you, I promise."

Julie tucks my hair behind my ear.

I get out of the car and lean down towards the window. I nearly say something. I nearly say, *Thanks, I know you want to help, it's not your fault*. I nearly tell her how I really feel and ask for help, but I can't quite do it. The weight of all that's happened is pushing on my chest. So instead I tap on the glass.

"Go easy on the mince pies, Julie," I say.

I turn and walk away.

Claws

*

Tom Becker

1 December

Exactly one year had passed since Holly had come back to the village. It had been a bleak welcome: grey, grainy skies; the rain's wet fingertips tapping on the windows of Gran's cottage. The small house was gloomy and unfamiliar, and coated in a strange smell that Holly would later learn was a potent brew of beeswax and mothballs. Old smells, from another century. The smell of her new home.

Gran had done her best to make her feel comfortable, chattering constantly as she led Holly through the cottage. The living room was dominated by a working fireplace, a brass coal scuttle filled with black lumps waiting beside the ash-flecked grate. A clock on top of the mantelpiece loudly doled out the seconds. It was surrounded by family photographs, a small gallery of fading ghosts and unfamiliar faces. As she stared at the fireplace, Holly had found herself wishing that it would swallow her up in its sooty mouth; that she could fly away up the chimney and melt into the sky like smoke.

A hand had fastened around Holly's arm. "Come away, dear."

It was Gran – a small, bird-like woman with glasses and tightly curled white hair. She was smiling, but her firm grip brooked no argument. Holly followed her out of the room and up creaking stairs to the attic, where her new room was waiting for her. The roof sloped down sharply over her head, a lone window offering a view of the flat expanse of fields. The floorboards were cold through Holly's socks.

"I hope this will do," Gran had said. "I know it's smaller than you're used to, but we'll make the best of it we can."

She patted Holly's hand and smiled encouragingly. Part of Holly had wanted to cry, but she'd told herself back in London that she wasn't going to do that any more. So instead she lay down on the bed and stared up at the roof, thoughts of the fireplace and Gran's tight grip drifting away.

She would remember, though – later.

2 December

Winter had come late to the village, only to arrive with a bite sharpened by hunger. The summer had been generous and warm, and it had been October before the trees let slip their leaves and autumn bonfires singed the air. Birds arrowed across clear skies in formation; fields hardened into barren furrows. The clocks went back. Nights drew in.

3 December

It was Friday morning: Mart had a dentist's appointment, so Holly sat on her own as the school bus rattled through the countryside. Trees looked like skeletal hands through the frosted windows. Breath blossomed into white clouds. Holly shivered and bunched her hands in her jumper. Behind her, the Marshall twins were bickering about who would get what for Christmas, while Fran and Kayleigh giggled and whispered. No one sat near Holly.

Right from the start, she had struggled to fit in. Two weeks after returning to the village, Holly had received an anonymous invitation through her letterbox, ordering her to wait beneath the elm tree on the green at sunset. The flowery message hinted at some kind of initiation rite, giving Holly a vision of circles of cross-legged girls, needle-pricked thumbs and solemn vows of friendship. Wrinkling her nose, she had tossed the invitation in the bin. Months later, she had learned that Fran and Kayleigh had waited an hour on the green before giving up. It had been Mart who told her, of course. By that point he was only person left in the village who wanted to be her friend.

Holly might have been born in the village, but having moved away when she was four, she would always be an outsider. Narrow lanes bred narrow minds, her mum used to tell her. Holly guessed that was why they had gone to London in the first place. But then her mum had died in a road accident, vanishing in a fog of exhaust fumes and traffic horns. Winter had once promised presents beneath the Christmas tree, and the possibility of snow. Now it brought only an icy reminder of what Holly had lost.

Nobody said anything to Holly about her mum, or about their time in London. Nobody seemed to say anything round here, but it didn't stop everybody knowing everybody else's business. It was as if the villagers had some ancient and arcane way of passing on secrets without words – smoke signals rising up from the chimneys, or coded arrangements of twigs in the woods.

At the back of the bus, Fran and Kayleigh burst out laughing: nasty laughter, like a sour chime of bells. The window gave Holly an icy kiss as she rested her head against the glass and closed her eyes.

4 December

"Go on," said Mart. "I dare you."

Holly gave him a withering look. "You *dare* me? You're such a child, Mart."

"You're just saying that because you're scared."

"Am not."

"Am, too."

They were standing at the gates of a rundown house on the edge of the village. It was fashioned from red bricks and boarded-up windows, chimneys poking up from either side of the black-tiled roof. A wooden fence laced with barbed wire marked off the scrubby garden out front. It was known as the Piper house, even though no one called Piper had lived there for years. Then again, neither had anyone else.

Mart adjusted his glasses as he stared up the path. He was two years younger than Holly, but his serious, deliberate manner made him seem almost middle-aged at times. Even his name sounded old.

"There's no such thing as ghosts," Holly said firmly. "You die, and that's the end of it."

"Rob Youds said his brothers came down here from the farm one night and saw her in the window," Mart countered, blinking owlishly.

"Rob Youds is an idiot. And so are his brothers."

"Prove it. Go take a look around."

Holly checked the lane was empty and pushed open

the gate. It gave way with a rusty squeak. The path seemed to lengthen as she walked it, the shadows deepening. Holly had planned on ringing the bell, but when she reached the front door she decided against it, gripped by the sudden fear that someone might actually answer. Instead she went around the side of the house and found a window where the board had come away. Cupping her hands against the glass, Holly made out a bare room with a wooden floor and a mirror above a large marble fireplace. Years of rumour and neglect had given the atmosphere a sullen edge.

Holly looked back towards the front of the house and saw Mart fidgeting anxiously at the gate. A gust of cold air blew her fringe in her eyes. She brushed it aside.

Something moved inside the Piper house, a black blur flitting across the hearth. Startled, Holly peered back through the window. It had happened so quickly that she was already doubting if she had seen anything at all, or whether it had been a trick of the light. Now, as she examined the room more closely, Holly saw that the walls were covered in marks – deep, spiteful scratches covering their length and breadth. It looked as though a wild animal had been trapped inside.

Holly backed away from the window and walked along the path as slowly as she dared, relieved when she felt the shadow of the Piper house release her, and the sunshine on her neck once more.

"What's up?" Mart said eagerly, when she reached the gate. "You saw something, didn't you?"

"It was nothing," she replied.

"I don't believe you. You saw Gwen, I know it."

"Shut up, Mart," said Holly.

5 December

After Sunday lunch, Holly and Gran washed up the dishes together. As she dried the cutlery, Holly gazed absentmindedly out of the window across the fields that ran behind their house beneath a vast, grey sky.

"I heard you and Martin were playing outside the Piper house yesterday," Gran said.

Holly rolled her eyes. "We weren't *playing*, Gran. We were just … there."

"Call it what you like," Gran said, handing her a wet plate, "but I call it trespassing, and so do the police."

"Trespassing? All I did was look through a window!"

"You stay away from that place." Gran's voice was sharp. "I won't tell you again."

She plunged a roasting dish into the water, inadvertently splashing Holly. In the year they had lived together, this was as close as they had come to fighting. One of them would always back away before they fell out properly, retreating upstairs or into the next room. Arguments were cliff faces: both of them were fearful of what would happen if they fell off.

Holly looked back to the window. "You think it might snow this year?"

"I hope not," Gran said briskly. "Hard enough getting around as it is."

Something in her tone told Holly that the conversation was over, and they washed up the rest of the dishes in silence.

6 December

That evening after school, the villagers filed through the darkness towards the church. Inside, the nave had been lit with candles, creating a cavernous hall of shifting shadows. Gran bustled along the busy pews, nodding to everyone she passed. When they finally reached their seats, Holly slumped down and folded her arms.

"I hope you're not going to sulk through the entire service, young lady," Gran said disapprovingly. "You can spare one evening a year for the sake of your grandmother."

"But does it really have to be *this* evening?" Holly groaned.

"It's the Advent service! It's tradition."

"So?"

It felt to Holly as though the village existed on some long-forgotten calendar, observing mysterious rites and celebrations from ancient times. Only that August, she had had to watch as Fran was crowned the Rose Princess and paraded through the village, glowing with triumph, on a chair carried by Billy Youds the farmer and his sons.

"Traditions are important," Gran said firmly. "They're like roots, stretching down deep into the soil. They keep us moored and nourished and safe."

"Safe?" Holly frowned. "Safe from what?"

A murmur spread through the nave, greeting the vicar as he stepped up to the lectern. He began the service by announcing that this year all the children of the village would receive the special gift of a Christingle. Holly had no intention of taking any gifts, special or not, but a sharp elbow from Gran jolted her from her seat. She sloped down the central aisle after the others: Fran first, naturally, followed by Kayleigh and the Marshall twins, a couple of the Youds family, and then Mart. The congregation's gaze felt like hot breath on Holly's neck, and in her haste to return to her pew she almost snatched the Christingle from the vicar's hand.

It wasn't until she was safely in her seat that she realized there had been a mistake of some kind. Her Christingle was an orange wrapped in a red ribbon – but instead of cocktail sticks with candied fruits, the fruit's skin had been pierced with five fish hooks.

"Eew!" said Holly, examining the sharp tips. "Is this a joke?"

"Hush now!" Gran told her. "Don't be so ungrateful."

Holly glanced over to where Mart was sitting with

his parents – he held up his Christingle, which looked identical to hers, and shrugged. Gran pursed her lips. The last thing Holly wanted was another argument, so she waited until they had returned home and Gran had gone up to bed before sneaking outside and putting the Christingle in the bin by the back door.

7 December

"OK, you win," Holly said finally. "Tell me about Gwen Piper."

She lay stretched out on Mart's bed, ignoring the unopened schoolbooks around her and gazing up at the model planets that hung like baubles from the ceiling. Mart sat at his desk, scribbling notes from a textbook. He paused, pushing his glasses up his nose.

"Not much to say," he said. "Years ago she went to the pond on Christmas Day and never came back."

"That's it?"

He shrugged. "People get a bit funny when her name comes up. Like it's bad luck or something. Did your mum ever talk about her?"

Holly shook her head. "Why?"

"I think they might have been the same age. Maybe she knew her."

"Mum never really talked about this place much. A bit about Gran, and Granddad when he was alive. But no one else." She rolled over and propped herself up on her elbow. "It was you, wasn't it?" she said. "You blabbed about the Piper house. That's how Gran found out."

Mart looked sheepish. "I didn't know *she* would find out. But you saw Gwen Piper, Hol. It's pretty big news."

"I told you I didn't know what I saw," Holly said stubbornly. "It was barely even a shadow. It could have been anything."

"So why are you asking questions about her?"

"Because I know Gran won't say anything, and you're the only other person in the stupid village who talks to me."

They both fell quiet.

"At church I heard Dr Marshall tell my dad he was going to take the twins away for Christmas," Mart said eventually.

Holly lay back on the bed. "So? It's a free country, isn't it?"

"It was the way he said it, I guess. Not like he wanted to go on holiday." Mart glanced over at the Christingle resting on top of his chest of drawers. "Like he wanted to get out of here."

8 December

Clouds gathered above the village, grey and swollen like bruises. The air turned bitter. In the lanes, people glanced up to the skies as they hurried home.

9 December

The snow fell overnight in a thick, silent avalanche. Sparkling white crusts formed on the hedgerows. The local pond iced over into a perfect mirror. Up in the rafters of Gran's cottage, the heater in Holly's attic room wheezed helplessly in the face of the cold. Even with thick socks on and the bedcovers tucked up over her head, Holly couldn't get warm. Finally she forced herself to get up and scurry over to the wardrobe, where she knew there was an extra blanket. Her clothes hung neatly on the hangers, arranged with a grandmother's care. Holly pushed aside the chequered curtain of school blouses, and froze.

The Christingle was hanging from the clothes rail by its red ribbon, the sharp fish hooks gleaming in the darkness. Gran must have found it in the bin and brought it up here. Muttering to herself, Holly went to untie the ribbon, but her fingers paused around the knot. *Traditions are like roots*, Gran had told her, back at church. *They keep us moored and nourished and safe.*

Holly grabbed the extra blanket and shut the wardrobe door, leaving the Christingle where it was.

10 December

The next morning Holly woke to find she had slept through her alarm. She stumbled downstairs, struggling into her school jumper, her hair still damp from the shower. Gran was sitting silently at the kitchen table, nursing a steaming cup of coffee. The snow had painted the window a pure white rectangle.

"I know, I know, I'm late!" Holly groaned. "You don't have to say anything."

"There's no school today," Gran told her quietly. "They didn't get the gritter out in time. The village is snowed in."

Her shoulders sagging with relief, Holly stopped wrestling with her jumper and sat down at the table. A plate of buttered toast was going cold in front of Gran, but she seemed to have forgotten it was there.

"Everything all right, Gran?" Holly asked.

"I'm fine, dear," she said, with an attempt at a smile. "Just tired, that's all."

Holly reached over and took a slice of toast. "You get up too early."

"You're young, dear. Sleep comes easily to you."

"Hey, I get stressed, too, you know!" Holly said. "I'm not a baby."

"You think you've got troubles," Gran murmured, cupping her wrinkled hands around her mug. "Wait until you get to my age."

11 December

Saturday. Holly's boots bit into the snow as she walked through the village, the winter air feasting on the tips of her nose and ears. At the green she heard laughter, and spotted Fran and Kayleigh walking towards the frozen pond. Their arms were interlinked, ice skates slung over their shoulders. Holly went in the opposite direction, up the hill towards the church, where Mart was waiting for her.

"I got your message," she said. "What's the big emergency?"

He turned without a word, leading her through the gate into a silent, snowy graveyard. Bare, low-hanging branches pointed accusingly at Holly as she passed. Mart carefully followed a solitary trail of his own footprints to the railings at the edge of the graveyard, where a pair of headstones were planted side by side in the ground beneath a silver birch. The first belonged to Gwen Piper; the second had been recently brushed clear of snow, revealing a name and two dates. Holly crouched down beside the headstone and examined the etched lettering.

"Evan Piper?" she said. "Who's that?"

"That's what I was wondering," Mart replied. "Gwen's dad, maybe?"

Judging by the date of Evan Piper's birth, he was certainly old enough to be a father. When Holly checked the date of his death, she looked back to Gwen's headstone, frowning.

"That's weird," she said. "Evan died a year after Gwen, on the same day: December 25."

"Merry Christmas," Mart muttered ghoulishly.

A rook cawed loudly nearby, startling them both. Looking up into the tree, Holly noticed something hanging from the branches. A wreath was suspended from a length of twine high above the graves: a circle of holly leaves with blood-red berries, blackened twigs poking out of it in the shape of a star.

"What's that doing up there?" breathed Mart.

"How should I know?" Holly retorted irritably. "I didn't put it there."

"Well, *someone* did."

They stood and watched as the wreath turned in the wind, a slow circle of tightening twine.

12 December

While Gran was at church, Holly dug out a box of old Christmas decorations from the cupboard, balancing precariously on an armchair to hang tinsel and paper chains around the walls. She even found a tatty plastic Christmas tree, which she placed proudly in the centre of the table. By the time she had finished, it was almost midday. Gran came back soon after, muttering to herself as she stamped the snow from her boots on the kitchen mat.

"Ta da!" Holly said, throwing out her arms.

Gran looked around the room.

"Well, what do you think?" Holly said.

"It's fine, dear. But you needn't have gone to so much trouble."

"We didn't do anything to celebrate last Christmas," Holly said. "I thought this year we could do with cheering up."

Gran toyed with the star on top of the plastic tree. "You're a good girl," she said finally, smiling. "It looks lovely. Now let's put the kettle on, I could murder a cuppa."

13 December

The lanes were still clogged with snow, so school was closed again. That evening Gran went to bed early, leaving Holly curled up in an armchair reading. She woke up to find the book resting half-open in her lap. The fire had gone out and the room had melted into darkness. Rubbing her eyes wearily, Holly closed her book and threw her blanket to one side.

As she stood up, she realized what had woken her: a loud scratching sound coming from the brickwork above the hearth. Holly wondered whether it was another bird. Over the summer, a young starling had fallen down the chimney and become trapped, and it had taken hours to get the distressed creature free. Holly went over to the fireplace and leaned over the ashen hearth, turning on the light on her mobile. The chimney was a black chute, acrid with soot. Arching her neck, Holly held up her phone and peered into the flue.

"Hey, Mr Birdie," she called out. "Where are you?"

A pair of narrow eyes stared back at her.

Holly screamed. Her phone fell from her hand. She bent down and snatched it out of the hearth, brushing ash from the screen and shining it back into the chimney.

"Holly?"

She whirled round to see Gran in her slippers and dressing gown, framed by the light in the doorway. "Whatever are you doing?"

"I – I fell asleep," Holly stammered. "There was a noise in the chimney, and when I looked up there, I thought I saw something."

"What nonsense!" Gran scolded. "You were still dreaming, no doubt. Come away from there and go upstairs, it's past your bedtime."

She was talking to her like she was a little girl, but for once Holly nodded meekly and did exactly as her gran told her.

14 December

Holly and Mart were standing beneath the elm on the green when Dr Marshall's 4x4 barrelled past, charging into the lane leading out the village. The big vehicle only made it a few metres before becoming becalmed on the white drifts. Wheels spun helplessly in the snow. Across the village, doors began to open, drawn by the noise. Holly tucked a stray lock of hair behind her ear and thrust her hands in her pockets.

"Didn't you say he was going to take the twins abroad?" she said.

Mart nodded. "Then the snow came. No one's going anywhere now."

A group of villagers had appeared with shovels to help dig the vehicle out, but Dr Marshall was still jamming his foot down on the accelerator, trying to force the 4x4 forward. Over the snarling engine, Holly could hear the twins shouting to be let out of the car.

"I thought I saw something last night," she told Mart. "At Gran's."

"Maybe Gwen Piper wants to make friends."

Holly punched him in the arm.

"Ow!"

"You're not funny," she said. "And what I saw wasn't friendly."

Mart nodded at the 4x4. "Why else do you think he's trying to leave?" he said.

15 December

That night the wassailers came forth, swathed in thick black cloaks and carrying bells and torches. They carved a fiery path through the village, singing and banging on doors, urging people from their homes. When Holly and Gran emerged, they were swept up by the procession. The carols sounded richer and darker than they had the previous year, solemn echoes from an earlier time – 'Good King Wenceslas', 'God Rest Ye Merry Gentlemen', 'I Saw Three Ships'. Gran slipped her hand in Holly's and gave it a squeeze, keeping hold as the procession snaked through the lanes on to the village green.

They came to a halt beneath the boughs of the elm tree, a large, torch-lit circle forming around its mottled trunk. The carol ended and another song began – a melody Holly didn't recognize, sung in a tongue that barely resembled English. An older song, a song of the soil. The hairs on Holly's arms stood up as the voices of the wassail rose to meet the keening wind. There was a movement on the other side of the tree and the ring parted to reveal Fran. She was dressed in a similar gown to the one she had worn as the Rose Princess, only this one was a deep crimson, and there was a crown of holly upon her head. Bells rang out across the green as Fran stepped forward, biting her lip. Billy Youds, white-haired and broad-shouldered, gravely handed her an ornate silver wassail cup. Fran pressed the cup to her lips and drank, liquid spilling down her chin and leaving a black trail upon her gown. She continued to gulp until the cup was empty, gasping when she was done.

Around Holly people were clapping and cheering, but all she could do was stare at Fran, who looked almost dazed as she handed the cup back to Billy Youds. The old man raised it up to the skies and the wassailers joined in song once more.

16 December

When Gran went to visit a friend in the afternoon, Holly huddled beneath a blanket on the sofa and watched TV. Flicking through the channels, she came across a Christmas film in which a boy was left alone in his family's house and had to defend it from a pair of burglars. He fought them off with a series of ingenious traps and was safely reunited with his parents. As the credits rolled, Holly looked around her living room and wondered what she would do if someone tried to break in. Would she hide in the cupboard under the stairs, or grab the heavy poker by the fire to defend herself? But the thought only drew her eyes back towards the chimney, and Holly was glad when she heard the back door open and Gran call out hello.

17 December

"What is it, Mart?"

He had called round in the middle of dinner, much to Gran's annoyance. As Holly stood in the hallway, she could hear the peeved scrape of cutlery across a plate from the dining room.

"I went back to the graveyard," Mart said, fidgeting with a toggle on his duffel coat.

"Well done you. See you tomorrow." Holly went to close the door.

"Wait!" he hissed. "There are five more!"

Holly frowned. "Five more what?"

"I checked the other headstones. Since Gwen and Evan Piper, five more people have died on Christmas Day. That makes seven in thirty years!"

The door to the dining room creaked open. Holly heard a loud harrumph.

"You're freaking out over nothing," she told Mart quickly. "It's just a coincidence. It's winter, right? Lots of old people die in winter."

"That's the thing – they weren't old people. I checked their ages on the headstones." His voice dropped to a whisper. "They were our age, Hol, all of them!"

18 December

In her dreams, Holly found herself walking down a long dark corridor lined with identical doors. She stopped by each one in turn, counting twenty-four until she came to one scored with deep scratches. Her heart thudding painfully in her chest, she realized it was her own wardrobe door.

Holly sat bolt upright in her bed, her skin drenched in sweat. She glanced across the dark attic room towards her wardrobe, and was relieved to see that the door looked the same as always. But it was still a long time before she fell asleep again.

19 December

A hoarse yell jolted the village from its wary vigil. Racing to the window, Holly saw Rob Youds running through the snow towards Dr Marshall's house with a large bundle in his arms. He was calling out for help. Holly slipped on her boots and ran out of the front door, almost bumping straight into Mart. He was out of breath, his face pale.

"What's going on?" Holly asked.

"It's Fran," he said, gulping for air. "We were out by the pond and one minute she was skating and then, *crack*, she was gone. Rob went over to help, but Fran was splashing and screaming and it took him ages to pull her out. Her skin had turned grey and I don't know… I don't know if she was even breathing."

Holly glanced back towards the doctor's house. Rob and Fran had been ushered inside by Mrs Marshall, a concerned crowd already gathering by the front door.

"It'll be OK, Mart," Holly said. "You'll see. It was just an accident."

"Says you."

Holly gave him a sharp look. "What do you mean? She fell through the ice, right?"

Mart shook his head. "You don't understand," he said. "Rob had Fran by the hand and he was pulling as hard as he could, but he couldn't get her out. She was bobbing up and down in the water, but it looked like…"

He trailed off.

"It looked like what, Mart?"

He pushed his glasses up his nose. "Like something had hold of her," he said quietly. "Something that didn't want to let go."

20 December

It was as if the crack in the ice that had appeared beneath Fran's feet had carried on into the village.

There were bitter arguments in the street; in the local pub that night, two men came to blows. Fran remained at Dr Marshall's house, suffering from shock and pneumonia. Holly heard a rumour that Billy Youds went back to the pond after dark, carrying a shotgun. But if something had been in the freezing water with Fran, it had long since gone.

21 December

Holly and Gran arrived for the evening carol service to find the church deserted, empty pews stretching out like a ribcage. They took a seat at the front, huddling together against the cold. Gran fished out a couple of wrapped sweets from her pocket and offered one to Holly. Several minutes went by before anyone appeared, and then an elderly couple eased themselves into the pew behind them. Every cough, every shuffle echoed in the silence. Eventually the choir came out and performed in front of the meagre congregation, filling the nave with their spiralling voices. Afterwards Holly took Gran's arm and they made their way home slowly through the snow.

Gran unlocked the back door and immediately went to put the kettle on. "It's bitter out, tonight," she said, rubbing her hands. "How about a hot drink?"

Holly went through into the living room and switched on a lamp.

"I'm OK, thanks!" she called back.

And stopped in her tracks.

There was soot on the carpet, a thin black trail leading straight from the hearth to the door. The wind let out a thin moan down the chimney – in Holly's mind's eye, a pair of narrowed eyes stared at her through the darkness. In the kitchen Gran was humming away to herself, the kettle on the hob whistling along in a merry accompaniment. Holly stopped herself from going through to tell her. It was just soot, no need to frighten Gran. Not yet.

The trail led out into the hallway, snaking up the steps towards Holly's room. The walls seemed to close in around her as she crept up the stairs, casting hesitant glances back towards the lights downstairs. She pushed open the door. Moonlight was flooding in through the window, drenching her room in a milky glow. Everything was how she had left it – there were no threatening shadows lurking behind the door or beneath her bed. The trail of soot had come to an abrupt halt. Holly sank down on her bed and let out a deep sigh of relief.

Gran's voice floated up the stairs, calling her name. She rolled over, but her reply died in her throat. The wardrobe door was ajar, the handle stained black in the moonlight. Holly ran over and flung open the door, peering inside. Nothing but piles of neatly folded clothes. She pushed aside her shirts on the rail.

The Christingle was gone. In its place hung a single ice skate, strung up by the laces. Its blade glinted wickedly in the light.

Like something had hold of her, Mart had said about Fran. *Something that didn't want to let go.*

Holly slammed the wardrobe shut and slumped into a ball in the corner of her room, burying her face in her hands.

Which was how Gran found her, minutes later.

22 December

"I'm so sorry, my love."

The two of them sat in the living room, nursing mugs of hot sweet tea. By now it was nearly one in the morning. Gran's face was drawn as she gazed into the fire dwindling in the hearth.

"I suppose I always knew you'd find out some day," she said. "But I wanted to keep it from you for as long as possible. The fear, I mean. I've been living with it for so long, I wish he had come for me."

"Evan Piper, you mean," Holly said coldly.

"Evan Piper is dead."

"But *something's* out there, isn't it? Something bad."

For a time the only sound was the ticking of the clock. Then Gran got up and opened a drawer, handing Holly a creased photograph. A little girl in a snowy field waved at the camera, wrapped up in a woollen overcoat, scarf, hat and gloves. It was Holly's mum. She stood in the shadow of a tall snowman with a lopsided coal grin, who leaned precariously over her. On the other side of the snowman a second girl with pigtails grinned a proud, gap-toothed smile.

"Hello, Gwen," Holly said softly.

"She was a sweet girl," Gran murmured. "But not smart and strong like you. She couldn't bear the fact that the other children... I wouldn't say they picked on her, but they didn't want to be her friends. One Christmas morning, Gwen went out to the pond alone. No one knew whether the ice broke beneath her, or whether she chose to..." She trailed off. "Evan blamed the village for what happened. At the funeral he started shouting wildly: if only Gwen hadn't gone to the pond alone, if she had only had a real friend. We were all too shocked to reply – and in any case, what could we have said?

"After that Evan shut himself away in his house – wouldn't answer the door, became a shadow in the window. Then, the Christmas after Gwen's death, they found him. Evan had hanged himself from the elm on the green. He was ragged and dirty, his skin was covered in scars. He'd been ... clawing at himself. The grief."

Holly shuddered. "That's terrible."

"An absolute tragedy, my dear," Gran nodded. "But still we didn't understand. It took us so long. When one of Billy Youds's girls vanished on Christmas

Night, we thought she'd run away. It wasn't until later, when a little boy disappeared after Midnight Mass, that we realized something was out there... A hunter. Years would pass by without incident and we would tell each other it was over. But then another child would be taken."

"Why didn't you tell anyone? Why keep it a secret?"

"Because this isn't a man the police can arrest, Holly!" Gran hissed. "It's a beast, a monster. And on Christmas Night, it comes for the children. Your mother thought if she took you away, she might be able to save you from him. But when she died, I was all you had left, I didn't have any choice! I've been doing everything I can to protect you."

"Protect me?" Holly laughed incredulously. "How? By hiding oranges in my wardrobe? Singing carols? All that stuff with the wassail cup and Fran – what good did it do her?"

"You shouldn't mock things you don't understand."

"I know, I know." The words were sour in Holly's mouth. "It's all about traditions and roots in the stupid soil. But we're not talking about crops and harvests, are we?"

"There are different kinds of harvests," Gran said darkly.

23 December

Mart called late, just as a shivering Holly was burrowing deeper under the covers of her bed. She reached over to her bedside table and snatched up her phone, which was resting beside the photograph of her mum and Gwen Piper.

"Hey," she said quickly. "You OK?"

"I guess," he said morosely. "But Mum and Dad are fighting downstairs."

"What about?"

"They won't say. But Mum's scared something bad's going to happen. She wants to phone the police."

"Maybe that's not such a bad idea," Holly said. "Somebody's got to do *something*, Mart."

Over the phone Holly heard a distant shout and a glass smashing. Mart went quiet. She could picture him at that moment, swivelling in his bedroom chair, staring up at his model planets.

"Promise me you won't do anything stupid, Hol," he said.

Gwen Piper's gap-toothed smile beamed at Holly from her bedside table.

"I promise," she said.

24 December

The blizzard began around lunchtime on Christmas Eve, fat flakes tumbling down from an already darkening sky. The village huddled in silence. From her window, Holly watched the snow descend on deserted streets. Fires burned in every hearth, smoke rising up from the chimneys in silent, slender trails.

Gran did her best to put a brave face on things, tuning the radio to Holly's favourite station and making a Christmas buffet for tea. But neither of them were hungry. As night fell, the church bells rang out in warning. Holly could see Gran was fighting to stay awake, but she had stoked up the fire so much the heat was only making her sleepier. The crackling lullaby continued as the clock ticked on towards midnight. Finally, Gran's eyelids drooped shut, her chin slumping against her chest.

Holly waited until she was sure Gran was asleep before going through into the hallway and closing the living-room door behind her. Moving quickly and quietly, she put on a thick coat and boots and slipped out of the warm cottage into the night. The blizzard had stopped, leaving a perfect white carpet over the lanes. The air was sharp with cold. Lights glowed watchfully around the edges of firmly drawn curtains.

Holly hurried down the lane and past the green, trying to block out the image of Evan Piper's body swaying in the wind beneath one of the branches. She was doing her best not to think, not to question what she was doing, not to lose her nerve. In the distance, the Piper house gradually emerged from the darkness, its eaves sagging under the weight of the snow. Holly reached the gate to find it stuck fast – when she climbed over the fence she caught her jeans on the barbed wire, ripping them open.

She pressed on, skirting around the side of the house. The snow here had piled up into drifts, forcing her to wade through it. By the time she had reached the back door, she was out of breath. Holly tried the handle and found it open. A part of her had been hoping it would be locked, and that she would have to give up her plan and return to Gran's warm cottage. But there were no excuses now. Her heart thudding in her chest, Holly stepped inside the Piper house.

Somehow it was even colder inside than out. Holly edged through a series of dead rooms, the walls covered in faded bruises. Floorboards groaned beneath her feet. The building felt more than empty – hollowed out, somehow. Pressing deeper into the house, Holly tiptoed through a doorway and entered the room she had looked into three weeks earlier. Deep scratches disfigured the walls. The darkness in the hearth was as thick as tar. Crouching down, Holly took out the photograph of her mum and Gwen from her jeans' back pocket and unfolded it. She laid it carefully down in the middle of the fireplace.

"Here," she whispered. "Take this. You're not the only one to lose someone they love."

She stayed in a crouch, not daring to look up into the chimney. The house seemed to hold its breath. Then the chimney shivered, covering her in a light dusting of soot. From somewhere up inside the flue there came a long, shuddering sigh – to Holly's ears, the sound of something very old and very tired settling to sleep. A small smile crept across her face. She stood up and turned away from the hearth.

She was halfway out of the room when a harsh rasping noise stopped her in her tracks. Returning to the hearth, she kneeled down beside the photograph. Her mum and Gwen's smiling faces had been obscured by a black cough of sticky soot.

A low growl rumbled down the chimney. Holly's blood froze.

She turned to flee as something came down the chimney with frightening speed, like a worm emerging from a black burrow. A clawed hand shot out from the hearth and snatched hold of Holly's leg. She screamed.

25 December

26 December

27 December

28 December

29 December

30 December

Mart walked up the path to Holly's cottage and pressed the bell. It took an age for the door to open – Gran let him in without a word, shuffling back to the kitchen and sitting down at the table facing the window. White fields glistened beneath a clear sky. Mart hung awkwardly in the doorway, fidgeting with the zip on his coat. Silence enveloped the kitchen.

"You don't have to keep coming round, you know," Gran said finally. "There won't be any news."

Mart looked down at the floor. "I warned her not to do anything," he said quietly.

She nodded.

"Do you think she's still there?" he asked. "Inside ... that place?"

Gran didn't answer. She took a sip of her tea. Her skin looked grey in the sunlight.

"You can go up to her room, if you like," she said.

Mart hesitated.

"It's safe," she said. "Christmas is over."

He left the old lady staring out of the window and went upstairs, his trainers squeaking on the attic steps. An icy draught greeted him as he opened the door. Mart swallowed. Christingles were hanging down from the ceiling on their red ribbons, a dangling orchard of oranges with barbed fish hooks. He tentatively pushed through them, sending them swinging back and forth. The room felt impossibly cold.

Shivering, Mart retreated from the attic and closed the door. Behind him Christingles swayed slowly in the draughts – in time to the sound of a very faint but persistent scratching, as though made by someone very far away.

Christmas, Take Two

*

Katy Cannon

I stared out of the car window at the end cottage, lit up with Christmas decorations, and clocked the 'Santa Stop Here!' sign sticking out of the front lawn.

I wasn't Santa. I wasn't compelled to stop here. Right?

"I'm just saying, we could totally turn the car round and drive back home now. Claim we got stuck in the snow."

Mum responded to my perfectly valid and sensible suggestion with a snort that drowned out the Christmas music playing on the car radio. "Snow? Heather, it's barely drizzling."

"There's ice in it though, look." I pointed at a melting drop of sleet on the windscreen.

"I hardly think your dad would believe this miserable excuse for winter weather stopped us driving twenty-five miles to his new house."

"Tamsin's house," I corrected her. Dad's house was still technically our house. Our warm, cosy, familiar house in the city. Tamsin's cottage in the middle of nowhere was an unknown quantity. I mean, I'd only met Dad's new girlfriend twice.

Fiancée, my brain corrected me. She wasn't just his girlfriend now. They were *engaged*. Never mind that Mum and Dad's divorce was barely final. Dad had moved on. There was flashy jewellery to prove it.

"We've been spotted, anyway." Mum nodded towards the cluster of trees at the end of the row of three joined cottages, where a boy about my age held an axe over his shoulder as he watched our car. He had dark hair, curling too long over his ears, and an angry frown creased his forehead, like he didn't want me there either. Which was weird, because I had no idea who he was.

As I stared back, he turned away, slamming the axe down on to the log waiting below. Chopping firewood. Was that really a thing out here in the country?

"Is he one of your new step-siblings-to-be?" Mum asked.

More people I'd only met once or twice who were

now apparently part of my family. I shook my head. "I think he belongs to one of the other cottages."

The boy disappeared into the middle cottage, firewood in his arms. His house looked bare and dark compared to Tamsin's, which was lit up like, well, a Christmas tree, with icicle lights hung from the windows. The middle cottage, on the other hand, had only a tattered green wreath on the door the boy had slammed behind him. The third cottage had a SOLD sign outside and looked empty.

Tamsin's front door opened, the bright light from inside illuminating the grey afternoon. Dad appeared on the doorstep, complete with comedy Santa hat, beaming at me as he waved.

"We could claim there was an emergency and we had to leave," I suggested. "Quick, get your phone out. Make it look like someone's calling with tragic news."

Mum sighed. "Heather. Come on. We talked about this. I know it's going to be a little strange—"

"Properly weird," I corrected.

"Spending Christmas with your dad and Tamsin. It's going to be strange for me, too, not having you there at Granny and Granddad's tomorrow."

"So let's make a run for it! I'd rather be with you anyway."

Mum pulled a guilty face at that, but it was true.

I didn't *hate* my dad – not like Lily hated her dad after he ran off with our maths teacher, Mrs Fletcher, and her mum had a mini-breakdown – I just didn't want a new family. I wanted my old one back.

Mum and I had done presents and turkey and stupid paper hats the day before, but it hadn't felt real. How could it? It was a fake Christmas so I could pretend I didn't have to spend the real one with my fake family.

"I'll see you in a few days, love." Mum gave me a quick hug and a kiss, and tried to smile. I didn't bother.

"See you, then," I said, pulling the door handle.

"I love you," Mum called after me, and I paused, swallowing hard as I nodded to show her I'd heard. I couldn't say it back. My throat felt too tight.

"My Heather-bear! You're here!" Dad stepped forward, the bobble of his Santa hat swaying in the breeze, his arms open wide.

Behind me, I heard Mum's car pull away. I was officially stranded.

"I'm here," I said, smiling weakly.

"Come on in, come in." Dad waved excitedly towards the front door. "Everyone is so pleased to have you here!"

I wondered if that was true. Dad was, obviously. But what about the family I was invading? I knew Tamsin's sons wished I wasn't going to be there – I'd heard them whining about it when Dad had called to arrange my visit. He'd hurried into another room pretty quickly, but it hadn't been fast enough.

I hadn't been able to make out Tamsin's response to their whining, but I could imagine it. I had to be there to keep Dad happy. That was it. No one else wanted me there – it was all a show for Dad. So he could be *their* dad now.

Tamsin's house smelled of freshly baked cookies, cinnamon and pine needles – quintessential Christmas – but it still didn't smell quite right to me. Like it was a smell from a bottle, sprayed around to convince me everything was perfect. Except there were actual homemade cookies on the plate in Tamsin's hand as she walked out of the kitchen, beaming. And the huge tree in the hallway looked real, too.

"Heather!" She put the plate down on the hall table,

in between a bowl of cinnamon sticks and pine cones and a festive silver stag decoration, then wrapped her arms around me in a hug. I returned it half-heartedly. "We're all so happy you're here!"

She stepped back again. Her smile reached her eyes and everything, but I knew it was only because it made Dad happy to have me there.

I'd heard her, too, the first time we'd met, when she thought I wasn't listening. She'd asked my dad if I was OK, if I was always so miserable. As if life as I knew it falling apart wasn't reason enough to be a little unhappy. Besides, not everyone had a permanent smile as their default expression, like her. Both times I'd met her she'd smiled constantly. It was exhausting.

"Thank you for having me," I mumbled, because I knew Mum would want me to. What I really wanted to say would probably get me thrown out.

"Would you like a cookie?" Tamsin asked, and I struggled to muster up a smile of my own.

"That would be lovely," I said, choosing the one with the most chocolate chips.

At least if my mouth was full I couldn't say anything bad.

Dad took my bag to the spare room, which was all the way up in the attic. At least the cinnamon fug probably wouldn't reach that far. It was giving me a headache.

I watched him head up the stairs and, as he went, a thunder of feet came in the opposite direction. Swallowing my cookie, I braced myself for the step-sibling invasion.

Millie, Tom and Rob. Aged five, nine and sixteen respectively, if I'd memorized that right. Rob was the same age as me, for definite. Our first and only meeting was an awkward pub lunch where Tamsin tried to make cheerful small talk, Rob went on and on about some computer game, Millie said she didn't like my hair, which I'd worn in plaits, and Tom kicked me under the table. Repeatedly.

All three of them had the same dad, despite the age gaps. I thought that Millie was probably some last-ditch attempt to save Tamsin's first marriage. It hadn't worked, evidently, as she'd got divorced when Millie was a baby. I wondered how it felt to know you weren't enough to make your parents stay together. And then I realized I already knew.

Maybe Millie wasn't old enough to feel it yet, but

I was. I knew that my parents had planned to stay together until I got through my A levels, because they'd told me so. But obviously, something had changed.

Was Tamsin the reason? Maybe that was why she was so damn happy all the time – she'd got what she wanted.

"Heather's here, everyone," Tamsin said, her voice as bright as the lights on the outside of the house. "Christmas can start!"

Tom, Rob and Millie all stopped at the bottom of the stairs to eyeball me, the interloper in their midst.

"Hi, Heather," Millie said, giving me a quick wave.

"Yeah, hi," Rob added, quieter than I remembered.

Tom mumbled something similar, before adding, "Cool, cookies!" and diving for the plate.

Tamsin whipped it out of the way before he reached it. "After dinner," she said sternly. "You know the rules."

"But *she* had one." Tom glared at me, and I tried to brush away any incriminating crumbs without drawing too much attention to it.

"She's our guest," Tamsin said.

Millie frowned and replied, "But I thought you said she was family now?"

Rob rolled his eyes at her. I got the feeling he wasn't so keen on the idea of a new sister either, he was just better at hiding it. Or maybe it was the thought of a new dad he didn't like.

I could sympathize with that. I already had a mum, I didn't need an extra one. But at least I didn't have to live with Tamsin and her constant perkiness. These guys would have my dad around all the time, being their dad.

Instead of him living at home with us, being my dad.

"Anyway, it doesn't matter because dinner is ready," Tamsin said. "Why don't you all go and put your stuff away in the lounge, then sit down at the table?"

"We're having dinner? Now?" Rob asked. "But Owen's coming round."

Tamsin's perma-smile froze for a moment. "Again? Rob, this is supposed to be a family dinner for Heather..."

"Owen practically *is* family." Rob gave her a look I didn't quite understand and she sighed. "OK, set another place at the table, then." Rob vanished into the dining room and Tamsin turned back to the kitchen, leaving me alone in the hallway with the Christmas tree, wondering who Owen was.

While I waited for someone, anyone, to come and tell me where I was supposed to go next, there was a knock on the door. That would be Owen, I assumed. I waited a moment, but no one appeared. Maybe they hadn't heard it. Maybe they were expecting me to answer it.

I headed to the front door and yanked it open.

There, on the other side, was the guy with the axe from next door. Well, he didn't have the axe with him any more, but still. It was him.

"Owen, I'm guessing?" I said, stepping aside to let him in.

He nodded, eyeing me curiously. "Yeah. And you must be the new sister."

"Heather." I had a feeling that wasn't what Rob referred to me as, but Owen just accepted the information with another nod, moving past me into the hallway. I closed the door behind him, resisting the urge to make a run for it. "I understand you're joining us for dinner?"

He paused, just for a moment. "Am I? That'll be nice. You sound thrilled."

"Why would I care?" I said with a shrug. "The more the merrier, as far as I'm concerned." Especially if it took attention away from me and my interloper status.

"OK, then." He picked up a cookie from the plate Tamsin had left on the table and took a bite. I wondered if Tamsin would have stopped him, too, if she'd been there. Whether Owen was family enough to be scolded or outsider enough to get cookies. Maybe I'd find out over dinner.

Dad reappeared down the stairs, looking red-faced and puffed. "Right, that's your room ready," he said. "I thought the boys had got it sorted already, but… Anyway, it's sorted now." Which I translated as meaning that Tamsin had asked Rob and Tom to get my room ready and they hadn't because they hated me. Fine. "Hello, Owen. Here for dinner?"

"Apparently," Owen said, around his mouthful of cookie. But his eyes were still on me. What did he see?

"Dinner's ready!" Tamsin sang out as she came into the hallway, carrying a large dish.

Rob stuck his head out of the dining room and motioned for Owen to head through, which he did, just as Tom and Millie emerged from the lounge and raced in after them. Tamsin smiled at me, then followed. Dad ushered me in, but I hung back a bit, letting everyone else sit first to be sure I wasn't stealing anyone's place.

I knew I didn't belong here just as well as the rest of them. The only one who didn't seem to believe it was Dad. I'd make it through this holiday for his sake. He was happy and, despite everything, I wanted that for him. But I also wanted to see what this family I'd inherited was really like – beyond Tamsin's constant smiling. As I eyed Owen across the candlelit table and the chicken and leek pie Tamsin was serving, I realized I might have a way to find out. He was closer to the family than I ever expected to be, but not part of it.

Owen, I suspected, saw a lot more than people intended him to – I could tell from the way he watched everyone as they moved around the room, serving food and pulling crackers even though it wasn't Christmas Day yet. The expression on his face, it was more than just watchful. It was like he was absorbing the whole scene, taking in every tiny detail.

What *was* his story? I really wanted to know. If only because it was far more interesting than wondering how my new family really felt about me.

Tamsin sat down at one end of the table, opposite Dad, and smiled around at us all. "Oh, it's so lovely to have us all together for Christmas Eve!"

I glanced across at Owen, who'd sunk a little further into his chair, as if they might forget he was there if he was very quiet. He was bigger than Rob – taller and broader – but right then he was almost invisible. He'd managed to make himself disappear at the dining table.

As we ate I tried to keep up with the flying conversation, the in-jokes and the constant clamour around the table. Rob was back up to full volume, talking loudly about some film he wanted to see. As an only child, I wasn't used to so much noise at dinner. Dad seemed to be in his element, though, joining in without missing a beat.

"So, what shall we play after dinner?" Dad asked as we finished eating. He turned to me. "We always play a board game after a big family meal. Usually it's Sunday Games Night, but I think tonight counts, don't you?" I smiled weakly. Great. Board games. I couldn't remember the last time I'd played an actual game – and never with Dad. It wasn't our style. We were more movie-watching types. We used to shout warnings at the really stupid characters in horror movies.

But apparently Dad had changed. It was all about the board games now.

"Scrabble!" Tom yelled over Millie's suggestion of Snakes and Ladders.

"That's only for four players," Tamsin pointed out, shaking her head. "We need something we can all play."

"Does *she* have to play?" Tom asked his mother in a whisper we all heard.

I felt my cheeks flaming red, even as Tamsin shushed him.

"Cards?" Rob suggested. "You did say you'd teach me and Owen to play poker..." He flashed Dad a grin and Tamsin frowned, even though her smile didn't shift.

"Maybe not tonight, hey?" Dad said. "What about charades? I know it's not a board game, but it *is* a Christmas classic."

A Christmas classic was mince pies in front of *The Muppet Christmas Carol* or *Elf*. Not this forced family fun, this ridiculous attempt at the most Christmassy Christmas ever. I couldn't shake the feeling that it was all an act – a way to show me that Dad was better off now he had them as his family.

Was this really what Dad wanted? Was this really why we weren't enough for him? Because we didn't play *Scrabble*?

Suddenly I couldn't take it any more. My face felt too hot in the candlelight, my head pounding from the scent of cinnamon permeating every inch of the house.

Without even thinking about it, I pushed my chair back from the table. The chair legs scraped against the wooden floor and everyone turned to look at me. Even Owen, his eyebrows ever so slightly raised over pale blue eyes, had all his attention on little old me.

Great. Just what I didn't want.

They were all waiting for me to say something, to chip in, and all I could think was, *I don't want to be here.*

"I should … clear the table." I picked up my plate and reached to take Millie's from beside me, too.

"I'll help," Owen said, grabbing his and Rob's plates.

Tamsin beamed. "That's so kind of you both! I hope you lot are paying attention," she added, looking at her own children.

I didn't stay to hear their responses. Laden with as many plates as I could carry, I hurried out to the blissfully silent kitchen.

Laying down my pile of crockery, I rested for a moment against the cool counter and willed my head to stop spinning. But before I could even catch my breath, I heard Owen dumping his dishes beside my pile.

"You OK?" he asked. "They can be a bit…"

"Loud?" Except it wasn't the volume, not really. It was the way they had three conversations at once and still managed to follow all of them. It left me dizzy.

"Much, I was going to say. They can be a bit much. If you're not used to them, anyway." He hitched himself up to sit on one of the stools at the counter beside me.

"Just a bit," I agreed. "But you are, right? Used to them, I mean."

Owen shrugged. "I guess. Rob and I have been friends since we were little kids."

"He doesn't like me being here, does he?" Might as well be blunt.

"Probably about as much as you like being here."

I sighed. Who really likes being somewhere they're not wanted?

"It's just weird," I said.

"Yeah." And that was it. I waited for him to say more,

but he didn't. We just stayed there, in the quiet of the kitchen, not talking.

It was kind of nice.

Owen propped his elbows behind him on the counter, staring up at the ceiling, and I took the opportunity to study him without him seeing me watching.

The hair I'd thought was too long when I first saw him seemed to suit him now. It softened his edges somehow – the hardness of his jaw, the sharp line of his cheekbones. I couldn't see his eyes, but I knew from earlier how direct they were, how deep they looked.

It was weird, in a way, his being best friends with Rob. They didn't seem anything alike from the little I'd observed. Rob was talkative where Owen was quiet, outgoing where Owen was reserved.

"Hey, Mum wants us to fetch pudding and bowls and stuff." Rob appeared in the doorway and Owen's attention snapped back from the ceiling to his friend. Rob nudged him with his elbow as he walked past to the fridge. "Your fault, showing me up."

"Sorry, mate," Owen said, throwing a swift smile in my direction. It was secretive, like we shared something Rob could never understand – how it felt to be an outsider.

Owen got up and took a stack of bowls from Rob. As he passed me, he paused for a second, close enough that his arm brushed against mine. "You'll get through it," he murmured, before carrying on.

I watched him walk away, still feeling the warmth where we'd touched, until Rob said, "Are you coming?"

Back in the dining room, Tamsin dished out chocolate pudding.

"She's got more than me," Millie objected.

I held out my bowl to swap, but she pulled a face and held her own closer. I sighed.

"You've all got exactly the same amount," Tamsin said.

I picked up my spoon, focusing on my pudding, and tried not to wince or react at all when Tom's foot collided with my shin. It *could* have been an accident, I supposed.

I was not going to let them get to me. I wasn't.

But that didn't mean I had to stay here and take it either.

"So, did we decide what game we wanted to play?" Dad asked, sounding incredibly cheerful.

278

I wasn't used to Dad being cheerful. It felt weird.

"Actually," I said, looking down at my unfinished pudding, "I'm kind of tired. If you don't mind ... I thought I might go up to my room and get ready for bed. Maybe read for a while."

Dad looked up. "Are you feeling OK, honey? Do you want me to fetch you some paracetamol or anything?"

"We haven't even listened to my new Christmas CD yet," Tamsin said, looking disappointed. Around the table, though, my step-siblings were looking secretly gleeful.

"I'm fine," I reassured Dad. "Just ... tired. It's been a long few days."

"OK. If you're sure," Dad said, not sounding convinced at all.

"I am. Goodnight, everyone." I smiled around the table, hoping it looked sincere. "I'll see you all in the morning."

"Wait!" Millie jumped up, arms waving. "You haven't hung up your stocking! Santa might not come if they aren't all there!"

My stocking. It hadn't even occurred to me that with Millie in the house that would still be a thing.

"Um, I don't think I brought one. Don't worry. Father Christmas will probably just leave my presents at home with Mum."

Millie's face fell at that and Tamsin stood up, her smile looking strained finally. "Don't be silly, Heather. Of course he'll come here for you tonight! And as it happens, we got you a stocking to match the rest of the family, didn't we, love?"

Dad nodded and reached over to grab a bag from the sideboard. "Here we go." He pulled out a quilted tartan stocking with my name stitched across the top in silver thread.

"Want to help Heather hang it up, Millie?" he asked.

Millie nodded enthusiastically and raced out to the lounge. I took the stocking from Dad and followed.

In the lounge, a fire crackled in the grate – a real one. And on either side hung stockings – one for Tom, one for Rob, one for Millie – and an empty hook ready for mine.

"It goes here!" Millie pointed at the hook, then watched to make sure I got it right.

I had a feeling she was more concerned that everything was perfect for Santa when he brought her presents than she was about me getting mine.

"Great." I reached across and hung the loop over the hook, then stood back to look at them all hanging together. Like a real family. Weird.

Millie skipped off back to the dining room, asking again at the top of her voice about playing Snakes and Ladders. I watched her go, then headed for the stairs.

"Night night, Heather," Tamsin called from the dining room.

The others echoed her, and Dad appeared in the doorway as my foot hit the first step.

"Your room's up these stairs, then up the smaller stairs on the landing," he said. "You're sure you're OK? You don't want to stay up and play games?"

"Sorry," I said, with a yawn for emphasis. "I'm just really tired."

"Yeah." Dad didn't sound like he believed me. "Well, hopefully you'll feel better after a good night's sleep."

"I'm sure I will," I lied.

*

Of course, once I got up to my room, I was wide awake.

I changed into my pyjamas – my fleecy ones with

penguins on, because they made me feel marginally more at home – and sank back on to the bed to message my friends for a bit. But they were all busy with their families and couldn't chat for long. I pulled out the book I'd packed, but I couldn't get into it. There was no telly in my room, and only so long I could play games on my phone without getting bored, so in the end I gave up and turned the lights out, curling up under the covers and trying to sleep.

Maybe it was the strange room, or the single bed shoved under the eaves, or the way the window frame rattled in the wind. Maybe it was the laughter coming from downstairs. Or maybe it was just me, feeling lost.

Whatever it was, I couldn't sleep. So instead, I found myself listening.

I heard Millie protesting about having to go to bed, half an hour or so after I left. I heard the boys laughing, with Dad's deeper laugh in there, too. As expected, they were all having much more fun without me.

After a while, I heard the front door open and Rob call, "See you Boxing Day, yeah." If Owen replied, I couldn't hear it. Probably he didn't. He didn't seem like the sort to talk more than he had to.

I settled back against my pillow again and listened to the sounds of a household going to bed. Rob and Tom bickering as they climbed the stairs, their heavy footfalls thudding through the house. Dad and Tamsin talking in quieter voices, a low hum that buzzed in the air. Then the stranger, unfamiliar noises of the house – the clanging water pipes, the creaking floorboards.

Was everyone else asleep? I couldn't tell. But in the tiny attic bedroom, the air seemed to grow thicker and hotter as I imagined them all, happy and home and exactly where they wanted to be. While I was stuck up here, alone and miserable.

I threw off my blankets, got up and paced. How was I ever going to sleep in this strange, noisy room? My self-imposed exile meant I'd already been up there for hours and the walls felt like they were closing in.

Because it was in the attic, the bedroom had a skylight instead of normal windows, but the pitch of the roof was surprisingly shallow. Unless you were right at the edges of the room, it was still possible to stand upright. The skylight was even high enough that I needed to stand on the rickety old dressing table to shove the window open.

Beautiful cold air rushed around my overheated face and I pushed myself up just a bit further to suck it in, feeling my lungs coming to life again as I breathed in freedom. I'd felt like I was suffocating in that room, in that house. Out there, in the night sky, for the first time since I arrived, I felt like me again.

At least I did until a voice said, "If you're coming out, I'd bring a blanket."

I jumped, whacking my shoulder on the window frame as I turned to face the voice. There, up on the roof that joined Tamsin's house and his, was Owen. He leaned back on his hands, his ankles crossed, like lounging around on a roof was *perfectly* natural.

"What are you doing out there?" I asked, shuffling my feet around on the dressing table to get my balance.

He shrugged. "Same thing you are, I expect. Getting some fresh air."

"Escaping." Suddenly I realized what the look I'd noticed on Owen's face earlier was. It was desperation – the feeling of being hemmed in with no escape. The way I'd been feeling since I arrived.

But what made Owen feel that way? Why was he

escaping to the roof on Christmas Eve?

"If you're planning on running away, I should warn you that the nearest main road is three miles away."

"I'm not running away," I said hotly. "But I am coming out."

I don't know why I said it. I hadn't had any intention of climbing out of the window. But if he could do it...

I took a step higher, on to a small shelf above the dressing table, praying it would hold my weight as I grabbed the window frame and levered myself out until I could sit on the edge of the window. Owen watched, his face pale in the moonlight.

"I'll be honest, I didn't actually expect you to do that," he said, as I crawled across the tiles towards him, my heart hammering against my ribcage. He was right – it was cold out on the roof, but my fleecy pyjamas and thick socks kept the worst away. Owen was still fully dressed, in a hoody and jeans.

"Honestly? Neither did I." I sat gingerly beside him, taking care to balance my weight so I wouldn't topple off the roof. His hand brushed against my back, as if he thought he might have to catch me, and the surprise of his touch made me shiver.

"In fact, you're not much like I expected," Owen went on.

"Well, I didn't expect you at all." Why was he so chatty all of a sudden? He'd barely said a word all through dinner, but now he seemed to want to *talk*. Maybe it was the darkness, or the fact that I was in his space.

"Yeah. The extra not-a-stepbrother. I guess I didn't come up in conversation when they were persuading you to come here for Christmas."

"There wasn't much in the way of persuading," I said. "It was decided for me."

"Is that why you're so grumpy about it?" Owen asked. "Because you shouldn't take it out on Tamsin, you know."

"I'm not," I snapped. "And I'm not grumpy."

"Right." Owen surveyed me steadily. "That's why you went to bed at eight thirty."

"I was tired."

"And yet here you are. Up on the roof. At nearly midnight. With me."

"With you," I echoed, returning his stare. What *was* I doing up there? This was crazy.

But for the first time since Mum left that afternoon, I felt like I was right where I was meant to be.

"It must be strange, I suppose." Owen's gaze shifted away from mine and he changed position carefully. "Spending Christmas here, I mean."

"Yeah," I admitted. "It's... Everything's different. And I don't ... I don't *fit* here." Why was I telling him? Then again, who else was I going to tell?

"I don't think you're trying to," Owen said.

"*You* seem to fit in well enough," I shot back. "I mean, it sounds to me like you're round an awful lot."

"I'm Rob's best friend." He didn't look at me as he spoke, but I could see his fist clenching as he brought his knees up to his chest. I'd hit a nerve. "We hang out."

"Yeah? Because it seems to me more like you were avoiding something else, maybe." I hadn't figured it out before, but now it made total sense. Owen didn't quite fit here either – but I was sure he fitted here better than at home. Why else would he take such care to fade into the background, to not draw any attention? Just in case someone realized he was there and threw him out? Why else would he be hanging out on a roof at midnight on Christmas Eve?

We were both misfits.

"Maybe I am." He shrugged, his fingers relaxing again. "Don't think it's any of your business though."

"Perhaps it isn't. But…" *It could be*, I wanted to say. I wanted to have something *good* come out of my visit here. If talking to Owen was that thing, I'd take it.

He sighed. "Home… Well, it sucks, quite a lot. So I spend some of my time at Rob's instead. That's all."

"Sucks how?"

"My stepdad… Let's just say he's not like Rob's – like your dad, I mean. And I'd rather be up here freezing my arse off than in there with him tonight."

I bit the inside of my cheek, feeling guilty for pushing. I might not want to be here, might not *want* to be welcomed into Tamsin's house … but she had welcomed me, even if her kids were less keen. And maybe Owen had a point. Maybe I hadn't really tried to fit in either.

Time to change the subject. "So, what were you expecting, then?" I asked. "I mean, if I'm not what you expected…"

Owen shrugged, but his body seemed more relaxed than it had, now we'd moved away from the topic of his stepdad. He stretched out his legs again and his thigh pressed against mine, warm in the cold night. Despite the warmth, it made me feel odd. Like thousands of tiny snowflakes were landing on my skin.

Then he said, "Rob said you were sulky and difficult," and the moment was ruined. I shuffled across so we weren't touching any more. Rob had met me all of once – what the hell did he know? "But…"

"But?" I clung to that word. I *wasn't* sulky or difficult. I just… I had no idea how to act in this situation. How to suddenly be part of a new family.

"But I guess I saw something he didn't. At dinner, I mean. You didn't look sulky. You looked…" He paused for a moment, watching me, and I wondered what he saw now, out here in the moonlight. Then he said, "Lost, I guess. Like you knew you weren't supposed to be there, and were hoping no one noticed you were."

I couldn't help it – I laughed.

Owen scowled at me. "It wasn't that funny."

"It wasn't funny at all," I said. "It's just … I was thinking exactly the same thing about you."

"Huh." He looked away. "I guess you could be right. Maybe."

"So neither of us fit," I concluded, but Owen shook his head.

"You could, if you wanted to. Tamsin wants you to, and Rob and the others will come round soon enough. They're good people, really, once you get to know them. Me... I'll only ever be the charity case from next door."

"I'm sure that's not true." But I wasn't. I'd been there less than half a day. How could I know?

"It is. And that's OK. I'm lucky that they let me hang out there as often as they do. And it's not forever. A few more years and I'll finish school, move away, and I'll never have to see him again." He gave me a sideways look. "Same for you, I guess. I mean, if you really *don't* want to be part of the family..."

I froze at his words. I was sixteen and so fed up with other people deciding my life for me, I'd forgotten that soon it would be up to me to make those decisions. I could live where I liked, spend Christmas with whoever I wanted.

And I realized, suddenly, that if I had to choose ... I would want to see my dad at Christmas, whatever happened. Always.

Maybe next year I'd be with Mum, and come to Dad and Tamsin for Boxing Day or whatever. And maybe Christmas would never be the same as I remembered, and maybe I'd never really be at home here, but the opposite – to not be wanted or welcome here – that was unthinkable.

I glanced over and found Owen watching me. "So. Not so bad here after all?"

"I didn't say that. I mean, they wanted to play charades."

"They wanted you to want to be here," he countered, and suddenly I felt ashamed. Maybe Rob was right. Maybe I *was* sulky and difficult.

My face felt hot again, even in the cold air, and my head buzzed with Owen's words. I was all set to shimmy back down through the window and hide under my duvet until Boxing Day when his hand crept over mine, squeezing my fingers. That shiver I'd felt when we first touched was back – and multiplied. Like Christmas lights flashing up my spine.

"You'll figure it out," he said, his voice rough. "It's not easy, I guess."

"I want to do better at it," I whispered, and he nodded.

He let go of my hand and glanced down at his wrist, pressing a button to light up his watch. "It's midnight. Christmas Day."

"I should get to bed." I shuffled forward, inching down the roof in a seated position. Then suddenly, I felt my foot slip and I jolted forwards, losing my balance. The tiles grated against my legs and panic flooded my body until Owen grabbed my arms, pulling me back against him.

"Careful!" His mouth was right against my ear, and I could hear a hint of fear in his voice.

"Thanks." I told myself that my heart hammering against my ribcage was just because of my slip, but it might have had something to do with his nearness, too.

"Any time." He held on a moment longer, then shifted to help me down to my window. With him holding me steady, I managed to get my legs through the gap, feeling for the dressing table with my socked feet. "Got it?"

"Think so." I turned around so I could see him, kneeling over the window above me. His eyes were dark in the thin light, his hair falling over his forehead, and his lips were close. All I needed to do was stretch up on my tiptoes…

He met me halfway, his lips pressing against mine in a swift, soft kiss.

"Merry Christmas, Heather," he murmured, as he pulled away.

"Merry Christmas," I whispered back.

He gave me a quick smile, pushing the window closed between us before vanishing from view along the roof.

I sat down on the dressing table.

Well.

That wasn't how I'd expected this Christmas to go.

It took me a moment to stop replaying my time on the roof in my head and realize that there were new sounds in the house. Floorboards creaking underfoot – someone was moving about down there.

Of course. Father Christmas.

I bit my lip. It was Christmas. Time to turn things around. Decision made, I opened my bedroom door and tiptoed down the attic stairs.

Tamsin turned, eyes wide and present sack in hand. She looked tired and she wasn't smiling.

I took a breath and smiled at her. "Need a hand?

I ... I'd like to help."

When Tamsin smiled back, it was with an expression of relief that looked more real than anything else I'd seen since I arrived. "That would be lovely. Thank you."

Together we filled Christmas stockings, stacked presents under the tree and I took a large bite out of the carrot Millie had left for Rudolph. Somehow making it look like magic for Millie made it feel magical for me, too. Like Christmas should.

As I straightened one last present before we left, Tamsin paused at the door and looked at me. Not smiling, not pretending, just being.

"I really *did* want you here for Christmas, you know, Heather," she said. "Not just for your dad. I wanted you to feel welcome. I know it's not easy, any of this. But... Well, I'm glad you're here. That's all."

I met her gaze head on. "So am I."

And for the first time, I was.

When Daddy Comes Home

*

Melvin Burgess

What? Speak slowly. A what? A terrorist? Me? Oh, come on, do I look like a terrorist? But hey, how would you know? I could be in disguise. But look at me – I'm cool, so cool. That's a dead giveaway. When did you ever see a cool terrorist?

Right, where are we? Let's see. Control panel... It's no use shaking your head ... what's your name? What? Oh, the badge. Angela. Well, Angela, I've done my research, I know what a control panel looks like. Cooperation, Angela – that's the name of the game. The quicker I'm done, the quicker you're gonna be untied and out that chair.

Check list. Laptop, cables. Jar of deadly poison... No, just joking! Don't panic. You'll choke. Calm down. It's not poison, OK? I was joking. Breathe slowly. Big breaths. That's it. Is the gag too tight? Yes? Let's see...

No, it never is – you're lying. I don't blame you, I would in your position, too. But just bear in mind, you're being counterproductive here. You just added another few minutes to how long I hold you captive. See? That's how it works.

Right. Let's get to it.

On one level, I am a terrorist, I suppose. I mean, you are being terrorized at this very minute, right? But that's not why I'm here. Any terror caused is purely coincidental. We apologize in advance for any discomfort. There will be no casualties. I'm only here to right a wrong, honest.

I actually come from a very privileged background, would you believe. You'll know my dad, I expect. Mark Holloway? Of course you do – the papers are full of him just now. The big comeback, eh? MARKIE COMES HOME – *The Guardian*. RETURN OF THE PRODIGAL – *The Telegraph*. HERE COMES SANTA – *The Sun*. Well, what do you expect of *The Sun*? But the message is the same. After years unfairly cast out in the wilderness, maligned, imprisoned, despised, Mark Holloway is coming home to Downing Street. On Christmas Eve. You have to admire his politicking.

Here comes Santa, just like the paper says. The Christmas message. Joy and goodwill to all mankind. A time for giving, a time for receiving. That's the symbolism. Of course, he's been pretty quiet about the exact nature of his Christmas gifts to the nation so far. But the feelings of Christmas will come across, I can guarantee that.

Unbelievable, really, when you think that only a few months ago, dear old Dad was rotting in prison. Nobody thinks about that any more. I expect you can barely even remember it, right? The law for cash scandal? Remember that? Millions taken in bribes from big companies to make sure they got the big grants, the low tax breaks and the right laws. Remember? Good, Angela! Well done. How about that sex scandal. No? Those poor girls – forgotten already! Shame. But then anyway, he was framed all along, right? Ah, now you remember.

What a turnaround, eh? Did you see the Queen's broadcast the other night? Yes? Riding into glory, as the Queen so aptly put it. Parliament dissolved so that she can form a government of national unity with my magnificent dad at the head of it! Unprecedented –

but she had no choice, did she? Best man for the job. Only man for the job, when you think about it...

Here we go. Mainframe, hello! I'm in.

I suppose, Angela, the question you must be asking yourself is, how did the son of such a charming man, such a *very* charming and talented man, end up here in the centre of the National Water Supply Unit, fiddling with the drinking water in such a distinctly terroristic fashion? Odd, to say the least.

Hang on. This is a tricky bit. Need to concentrate. It wouldn't do for the sensors to pick up that some kind of alien material is coming into the reservoirs now, would it. And ... hey! Wow. Good news, Angela. For me anyway. This is some pretty old-fashioned equipment you have. I reckon with a little fiddling I could pour a whole tub load of rabies in here and the good folk of London would wake up foaming at the mouth and biting each other. Sorry! Joking again! Don't fret, Angela. Really inappropriate. I'm sorry. No disease going in here ... promise.

Ah! Hang on a moment. God. Ow. Ow! My head! Concentrating too hard, you see. This better be worth it. Je-sus! You know what they say – the truth hurts.

Well, they're bloody right. Christ. Ah! There, it's going. Intense, but mercifully brief. And you know what? There's nothing you can do to stop it once it gets hold. There. Gone. My God, when it gets hold of you though! You think your brain's being boiled alive.

Where was I? Oh, yes. Checking the input systems.

I bet I know what you're thinking, Angela. You're thinking – Mark Holloway! Great politician, lousy family man. Am I right? That's why I'm here, surely – because he was a bastard at home. Beat up my mum. Abused me and my sister. The old story, eh?

Listen; I can remember my dad reading us a bedtime story every single night when he was PM. Astonishing, eh? There he was, running an entire country – never cut down on his time with us. War in the Middle East? Sorry, it'll have to wait, my kids are halfway through *Diary of a Wimpy Kid*. Chinese President over for vital trade talks and then dinner at Buck House? Great! But I'll just have to nip home in between courses for chapter three of *Harry Potter and the Flying Pigs*, or whatever.

He even managed it when he was abroad. How about that? What a man. No, not Skype. In the flesh.

Must have got the RAF to jet him home just so he could read us a story. All the way from Australia and back in a single night, sometimes. Now that's what you call a dad, right?

What's that, Angela? Almost too good to be true, you say? But I remember it, I tell you! Clear as day! It's all in here, in my head. How could that be, if it never actually happened?

Yeah – my dad. Never let us down once in all those years. Not like our mum. What a cow she was! Do you remember that? It was all over the press at the time. Of course you remember that! Poor old Markie. I know he always said it wasn't her fault – typical of the man to be so generous, eh? Mental illness is a terrible thing. Fact is, though, she was a right cow long before her mind went. No, Angela – it's no use arguing with me. I remember. I was there. I know.

Right, right. I'm doing well, on time. Now for a little reprogramming...

I could go into more detail if you wanted me to. I remember it all so vividly. Like a film playing in my head. Dad, the loving, caring, responsible parent. Mum, the selfish waster. The affairs she had! I can remember actually walking in on her once, when she was banging some bloke – God knows who he was – and she offered to pay me £20 not to tell Dad. How about that? Me, me, me all the time with Mum, it was. All the good times were with our lovely, lovely dad.

Christmas, for instance. Ah, Christmas! Everyone likes Christmas. Do you like Christmas, Angela? You would not believe the Christmases we had when I was a kid. Of course, Mum always got drunk and started a row, if she was there at all, that is. But that didn't matter because Dad was there. Never mind the Queen. Never mind the pan-Asian alliance asking his advice. Never mind riots in Manchester. Always be home for Christmas with the kids, that was his motto.

It wasn't just me and my sister either. We had other kids round. Barnardo's. Homeless kids, abandoned kids, immigrant kids. They didn't know what hit them! Heaps of gifts. Feasts, fun and games. They were the most Christmassy Christmases anyone ever had.

Dad knew all about Christmas, I can tell you.

The Christmas fairy. Do you know about the Christmas fairy? Every year, Christmas Eve, the Christmas fairy appears, bobbing up and down in front of the door to the conservatory. The little kids are amazed! It's magic! Of course, she's just a handkerchief, rolled up and hung on a piece of thread running down the door and up my dad's trouser leg to his pocket. He's jiggling her up and down with his finger – but the kids don't know that. They believe it – every single time. Up and down, up and down, up and down.

Then Dad bends an ear to her and listens carefully… "What's that, Christmas Fairy? Santa's on his way, you say? Really? And … he's coming here now? Oh, did you hear that, children? Santa's coming to visit tonight!"

Then there's sleigh bells upstairs and a few minutes later the door bursts open – and there he is! Santa himself. My dad as well, of course, dressed in all the gear – red suit, big beard, bearing gifts and mince pies, laughing and joshing and chatting away to the Christmas fairy and her minder and being – well! Just being wonderful. I used to love those memories. Still do. Even though I know now that it's all really just a great bag of shit.

Did you spot what happened there, Angela? How Dad was Santa, but at the same time, in the same room, there he was jiggling about with the Christmas fairy and chatting to Santa! Like he was in two places at once. Gives a whole different meaning to talking to yourself, eh? But hey! That's old Markie Holloway, miracle worker. Two places at once? No problem! Let's make it three. All you have to do is ask...

Right, I've rerun the software. Now a little code... This is fun, isn't it, Angela? Oh ... come on. Please don't start crying. I can't stand it when girls cry. I'm such a softie. Here, look. Wiping your tears away, see? Being kind and considerate. Being gentle.

You're blaming yourself, aren't you? I thought so. I'm good on psychology. Look, it's not your fault! I had to get past several guards and all sorts of alarms and stuff – that's not even your job! I know, I know, it's hard to just sit here and watch me getting up to no good...

Except it kinda depends on your point of view, doesn't it? As far as I'm concerned, I'm actually doing a lot of people a great big favour here.

Have to hurry. Need to get this done before your co-workers arrive, eh?

I expect you're wondering what this is all about,

Angela. Well, I'll tell you. It's the truth. That's it. What's true, what's not true. And how can you ever tell in the first place? If we lose track of the truth, what are we? Or perhaps you're one of those people who don't care about the truth? Oh dear, panicked shaking of the head. Don't worry – you're entitled to your own opinions, I won't hold it against you. But the truth, Angela – the truth happens to be very important to me. I take it very personally indeed. You see, I happen to know that there are certain areas in which you and a great many other people in this country have been misinformed. And that won't do, it won't do at all. So I'm just … well, I'm just putting things right.

That's what's in the bottle, Angela. Truth. Dangerous stuff, truth. But it's going in the water supply, nothing you can do about that. Tomorrow morning, the nation will be supping it up in their morning cuppas.

Nanomeems. Heard of them? No? Something on the news a while ago, maybe? Never mind. Been around for a few years now. See, it's cloudy. That's because it's full of those teeny-tiny, itsy-witsy nanomeems. Billions of them. Literally billions. Water doesn't hurt them. Boiling can't touch 'em. Not even that miracle of nature, the human immune system, can get rid of them. Once you ingest 'em, you got 'em for life. They migrate directly to the brain and then ... well, they just sit and wait, sit and wait, until a prearranged cue sets 'em off. Could be anything. A sound. A sight. Mark Holloway in a Santa Claus costume, perhaps? How about that?

And then – off they go! Burrowing their way into the brain tissue. They migrate to the synapses and start work, closing down a few million or so here, opening up some more over there. Think of them as tiny memories, if you will, sitting in your brain, waiting to come to life. Because that's all memory really is. In some ways that's what we are – our minds, our personalities, even our feelings. Synapses. Some open, some closed. That's it. This little group is your memory of your auntie Mary. This group colours the way you feel about Uncle Simon that time he threw up at your birthday party. This group over here is the memory of your dad hitting your mum. For example. Get it, Angela? See where I'm going with this? Hmm?

There's a school of thought that states we are all no more or less than the sum of our memories. What do you reckon? True or false? Debate. Our entire history, our philosophy, our past, ourselves – it's all about memory in one form or another, isn't it. So tell me; if you can't remember something, how do you know if it ever happened? Because other people remember it, I hear you say? Correct! Good, Angela! Ah, but here's another thing. What if everyone forgets? Well, in that case, it might as well have not happened at all. Unless – what's that, Angela? Unless the information is written down or recorded in some way? Correct again! Good girl. Top of the class.

OK, let me ask you another one. What if everyone misremembers? What then? Suppose everyone remembers how Mark Holloway went to prison for fraud and various unnamed sexual misdemeanours? Hmm? But ... kind of only just. And ... it was a pretty minor thing, after all. OK, it's the PM getting sent to jail for fraud, but hey! These things happen, don't they? And instead of remembering what a complete fucking shit he was, they remember, say – that he was a bit of a lad. Those girls were just trying to make money out of the poor bloke and they were probably lying about their age anyway. That money he got – it was a mistake! And then, hey! It turned out he was framed all along anyway! How about that?

I see you shrug. Conspiracy theory, you say. Crazy guy getting convinced about crazy stuff. People change their minds all the time, so what? True, true, very true. So we changed our minds about my dad. Or else, someone changed them for us... Now who could that be, I wonder?

See how simple it is? A few synapses firing up here, a few more not firing there and hey presto! Everything changes. Markie Holloway turns overnight from zero to hero. Except – the truth is still the truth, isn't it, whether anyone remembers it or not. A lie is still a lie. Memory might be fallible, but the past – that never changes. Ever.

What's the time? Damn, got to get a move on. You are clever, Angela. Trying to delay me with all this chatter. Not much to do now...

Right, that's the sensor systems sorted. Next, the reboot. Oh, Angela, there you go again. Tears for souvenirs! Tell the truth, you weren't expecting that I knew about the reboot, were you? Oh dear. You do feel terribly responsible, don't you? There's you, nice girl, first job out of uni and suddenly here you are drugged, gagged, tied up and forced to watch some loony terrorist trying to destroy everything you hold dear. How very trying for you.

OK, let's get this system ready to accept the new input.

I was seven when Mum finally went mad. Must have been one of those unstable sorts, eh? Explains her selfish behaviour in some ways. She started getting all mixed up. Confused. That was the first sign, but it all happened very quickly after that. Within a few days she was remembering things that had never happened, forgetting things that had. False Memory Syndrome, they said. Next thing, her brains just scrambled. Bang. Almost overnight. I can remember how terrified she looked that morning. It was me who found her, weeping in the bathroom, poor thing. Couldn't speak, couldn't remember anything. She still knew who I was at that point, though. Held me to her and stroked my face and made these horrible, guttural noises. And me? I screamed and screamed for someone to come and get her off me. I find it very hard to forgive myself for that.

Two days later, my little sister. Same thing. Memories all scrambled up. Didn't know today from yesterday, Mum from Dad, up from down. Now, what are the chances of that happening, eh?

Yeah. I don't see them very often any more. They're in an institution. Doped up to the eyeballs. I can't bear it, to be honest. I mean...

*

Sorry. I'm OK, now.

Me? Thank you for asking, Angela. Sane as the day is long, except I did start getting these vicious headaches at pretty well same time. Coincidence – of course!

And no, in case you were worrying, none of you are going to have your brains turned to scrambled egg, you needn't worry about that. Amazing how fast tech develops these days, isn't it? It was only twelve years ago when Dad used Meem technology to change our memories. And now, well, now they can change the memories of the entire nation ... and no one even knows about it.

Angela! A thought's just occurred to me. I'm wondering if it could be that you've sat here and watched similar jars being emptied into the water supply. Could it be that you are – I hate to bring it up, but you never know – actually complicit in the rewriting of our recent political past yourself? Hmm? Well, well, let's not go there. But if you have, my dear, you can relax your guilty conscience. Because this jar, unlike any others that you may or may not have seen go into our waterways – this jar is the Truth. This is going to reverse everything. All the lies, all the inventions. Everything back to how it was. More or less. I don't know everything myself, of course – had to fill a few gaps, make up a bit here and there. But hey – that's the nature of truth, eh? It's an imperfect thing. I guess it always was.

What? Sorry? What? How do I know all this? Oh, right. I found the files. See, I work for him. Yeah, I know. I was lying about being cool. I'm actually a geek. A big one. Yep. A great, big, fat geek. I started getting flashbacks, that was the start of it. Double memories. That's weird, I thought to myself – how come it's both Mum and Dad sitting around opening presents with us on Christmas Day, when Mum was also spending Christmas in rehab? How come it's both Mum and

Dad kissing my knee better that time I fell off the slide at the local park. How come…

The flashbacks got worse. I put two and two together. I was working in Dad's office at the time, helping to coordinate his political rehab, so I did a bit of digging.

And guess what I found out? I found out that everything I remembered was shit. All of it. My entire childhood had been retooled to make that fucker look good. What do you think of that? He created this version inside my head, where he – the biggest, most absent, philandering, lying, unreliable and occasionally violent father who ever walked this earth – is turned into Mr Nibbily-Niceicles. And my mum, my poor, long-suffering mum, my kind, caring, doting, loving mum, who was always there for us, day and night, who did her best right up to the point where she could put up with him no more, was turned more or less into … him! Yes. A drinking, shagging, lying machine. My lovely mum. He did that to her. He turned her into him.

How about that? Can you imagine that? He destroyed his own family to make himself look good.

What's that? Why didn't I just publish the files?

I did! And you know what? No one took any notice.
Meems, you see. One of the easiest things to do is
interfere with the relative importance of things. The
PM sent to jail for fraud? Who cares! Destroyed his
family's minds with Meem tech? Nah. You'd have to
be crazy to believe nonsense like that...

Oh, Jesus, here it comes again. I get these headaches
like you wouldn't believe. Bad tech. Oh, God, that
hurts. Ow ow ow ow. They got even worse when I
reversed what they'd done to me. Reprogrammed the
Meems – it can be done. Resculpted the brain, put
back what had been changed. If I'd had just a bit more
time ... just a bit, I might have fixed it up a bit better.
Oh...!

There, it's going. Thank God. It's like cramps. All
you can do is wait for it to pass.

Yeah, well. I'm afraid you're going to find out all
about the headaches. My Meems are a little bit ...
kinda homemade. The Meems he used on me and
Mum and Val, they were pretty crap, and I had to use
his leftovers. 'Fraid so. Couldn't start from scratch –
didn't have the equipment or the skills. I had to do it
at home on my Mac, with a glass jar and a bottle of

rejects. Such is the nature of Truth. Whereas the ones he used on you and the rest of the nation, Angela, to reshape your attitudes and memories of him – that's a different ball game altogether. Of course he had a huge business consortium behind him by then. Billions of pounds … dollars, euros, yen, roubles, yuan. They're all in on it.

Right, I think we're ready. I'll just fix the jar in place. Final check…

Apparently Mum found out some of what he was up to, threatened to go public unless he gave her a divorce. Was prepared to do it quietly, but he wasn't having that. She wanted the kids, you see – no way was he having that! That might have a negative effect on his electoral chances. So he tried to change her mind instead. First, by argument. Then, threats. Finally, with Nanomeems. Failed on all counts. Tried to change Val. Failed. Managed it just about with me. See? I'm only a bit crazy. Don't you think? I do get a bit confused sometimes, but that's because I have two complete sets of memories in my head. One real, one fake. It's exhausting.

Still, it's a small price to pay when you consider

what a great boon to mankind Nanomeems have been. For hundreds of years politicians of all creeds have been reduced, entirely against their will, to lying and cheating in order to make sure we have a proper, professional administration. They don't have to do that any more, thank God. They just change the truth.

There! Away they go. Bye bye, little Meems! Into the water system. Over one hundred billion of them in that one jar. Amazing, isn't it? Like so many tiny sperms, fertilizing the heads of the nation with the Truth.

Of course, not everyone will get to see him in his Santa costume, but not many will slip through the net. It'll be all over the news, on TV, in the cinema. Magazines and newspapers. Posters on the street. And then – truth and headaches, Angela. Truth and headaches. Happy Christmas! Ho, ho, ho.

Tomorrow morning, when you turn on your TV, there'll he'll be, my dad in his Santa suit. What's supposed to happen is – Lo! Hope! Trust! Joy! The spirit of Christmas! All those lovely Christmassy feelings welling up into your hearts. Happy Christmas. Happy Markie Holloway! Good will and peace to all men! The Christmas spirit. Markie is coming home!

It makes so much sense!

See him lose an election after that? I don't think so!

But he's not Santa, is he? He's the Grinch. He stole Christmas off me and now he's trying to steal it off you as well. He's trying to steal it off every man, woman and child in the country.

You think I'm crazy, I expect. Well, maybe I am. But when you turn on your TV in the morning and see my old man in his Santa suit, or on the front page of papers, or on a poster as you drive back from your mum's on Boxing Day, it won't be Christmas joy you're gonna feel. It'll be disgust. Revulsion. Anger. A soupçon of hatred and bitterness. A sense of betrayal. By this time tomorrow afternoon, you won't be able to stand the sight of him.

There. I'm done. What can I say? Sorry I had to put you through this, Angela. Sorry about the headaches, too. Have a good Christmas – and don't forget to vote next time round. It's your say in the government of this country.

Bye!

The Bluebird

*

Julie Mayhew

This voice. Very quietly.

Let's start at the start.

It's winter. Moony night in a small town. Trainer-scuff black. Follow me, invisible, down to the Coke-bottle bobbing sea, past terraced kingdoms (with enchanted gardens just about big enough for the wheelie bins). See the cashpoint, charity shop, betting shop, chippy. Smell the beer-and-crisps lure of The Dog and Sparrow (but beware the troll who asks for ID). All about the town, lights are roped, more gaudy than a landlady's jewellery. Strings of treasure they are, a sign that joy is around the corner. Unless the way they wink only reminds you how distant life is from a Christmas-card scene.

Onwards we go, through golden ink spots dropped by lampposts, past doorways spilling real warmth and fake laughter. There's treasure afresh to be found as we near the suck and spit of the great grey ocean – treasure more valuable than starfish and seaweed, crabs and old shoes. The lights of the Magical Palace shine all year, whatever the season, yet still no one comes to this yawning, dumbhead town to play the amusements. People only come here to sleep. For this town is a home. And home is a place people go back to, not a place they head for in the first place. So take the advice of a resident – those grab machines in the Magical Palace will never reward you with what you desire. I've been trying to get me a bluebird for months now. Could have bought one outright five times over with the gold that machine has eaten.

Look, listen and cross the road. Step inside the Co-op on the corner.

See that girl with the long-long hair buying baked beans? She's called Rae. She likes a bit of Dylan Thomas, if you hadn't noticed. Doesn't mind a bit of Poe either, a Grimm tale or two. Books, basically. Stories and tales and songs and skits – the things we gift ourselves when the universe refuses to pay out. This girl, this Rae, you don't see her much, whether it's December-cold or the sun is sending ice cream running down your wrists. When Rae's not at school, she's locked in a tower. Some say it's an ogre that keeps her there. That's what they call Rae's dad. Though they don't understand. Ogres grow out of difficult situations. If your mum does a moonlight flit, leaving no word of explanation, it bends and shapes your so-soft dad into something seeming less human.

So look up, up, above the Magical Palace, above the coloured bulbs that are cursed to dance that sequence for eternity, and there you'll see it. The tower. The two-bed flat. The living-room windows, at least. The entrance is on the side street by the skip and the cobbles, and that's the view Rae has when she sings from her window. There are no tunes of jolly snowmen and candy canes and sleigh rides and bells. Not when Rae is doing the deciding. Judy knew how to tell it. All the right festive words – a gay yuletide, days of gold – set to a key that will break your heart.

But turn your gaze, for now, away from Rae and on to the boy in the Co-op confectionery aisle. Because he's the important one in this story. Watch as he zips a box of Ferrero Rocher inside his trackie top.

That's Ben, prince to Pregnant Tanya, and he's shoplifting only because it's bad luck to ignore the cravings of a girl who's expecting. Rae sees what he's doing – oh, she's observant as well as being lyrical – but she doesn't give it too much mind. If she did, she'd have to notice how Ben and Tanya are part of a gang, a family of sorts, made up of people a little bit like you but different enough to be different. People you choose. Ones you don't have thrust upon you. And noticing that would make Rae sad.

So she pays, leaves, doesn't let herself sigh.

*

She heads back to the two-bed tower as the cold-cold day turns into a freezing night. She upends those beans into a pan and serves them warm on toast to the friendly ogre, who is watching the snooker. Then later when Rae is in her room, singing Judy's seasonal, sorrowful song about faraway troubles, Prince Ben happens to be passing the Magical Palace. He hears our Rae singing that song, letting it drift down from her bedroom window, past the skip, across the cobbles, and he feels it enter his hard, hoodie-covered heart.

He stands, as if held by a spell, so that he might hear more. Though lord only knows why! Oh, Rae can sing sweet enough but – here she goes! – shifting into a new song, an unseasonal one, with words so sour – all about a bird breaking into a house and getting more than a broken wing for its trouble.

"Hey! Rae!"

The stone pings from the window and bounces into the rubble of the skip. The tune cuts. And there is Rae, long-long hair tucked for safety behind her ears, hanging from the window frame, peering into the gloom at the cobbles below.

"Whaddya want?" she says, not measuring out her words, even though this is His Royal Highness, Prince Ben of the seaside, stealer of Ferrero Rocher, breaker of hearts.

"You," he replies. "Come down here."

She scoffs. She splutters. "You've gotta be kidding!"

And Ben scoffs and splutters in return. He has never had anyone say 'no' to him before. He is struck dumb now, as well as still. He is struck fascinated.

"Me dad'll be done with his dinner soon," Rae goes on. "Then he'll need a cup of tea. And who'll be doing that if I'm gabbing on the street?"

"Well, he knows where the kettle is, dun't he?" says Ben, recovering his tongue.

"Yeah, but by the time he's got to it, he'll have forgotten what he wanted it for." Oh, it's so hard to explain to the ogre-uninitiated! "I just don't want him to have the stress."

"Oh," says Ben. "Oh."

"Oh," says Rae. "Oh." And though she has always known how to pitch a note to dismantle even the most vigorous of listeners, she had never before realized the power of her own speaking voice. That is, she had never really noticed what was in it – lurking, giving her away. There in that everyday melody, without her having to try, was an overwhelming sadness. She hears it as she sends words out to the prince below and she cannot pretend that he doesn't hear it, too.

"Oh, come on, Rae!" The prince begins his gentle begging. "Let your hair down. We all need to let our hair down every once in a while."

Maybe it was the timing, the position of the moon marking out the angles of his face, the clouds his breath made in the lamplit dark. Maybe it was a perfect alchemy of hormones and the upcoming holidays. Or could it have just been the distant promise of a stolen Ferrero Rocher. Whatever it was, just as her song had drifted down, Ben's words drifted up. Those words, they enter Rae's closed-off, cardiganned heart.

*

There was to be a day trip – a quest, if you like – to the next town, to see if it was as slow and black as the place they had always called home. To see how gaudy its Christmas lights dared to be. Rae is invited.

But she has been warned about villainous boys and witchy girls and the dangerous world outside their flat. The ogre is hopeless at making tea, but he is good at warnings. It would be a waste of hard-won time even to bother asking to go.

But every night, as the hush comes, Ben is there at Rae's window with words of persuasion.

"Come out, Rae, have some fun, let your hair down."

He even shins up the drainpipe, using the leverage of the lip of the never-emptied skip, and places an early Christmas gift on the peeling paint of her bedroom windowsill. It is a necklace – shiny and star-like, with a stone impersonating the beauty of a ruby – and it is the most brilliant thing she has ever seen. Treasure – maybe. She puts it on, looks at herself in the mirror and catches a glimpse of who she might turn out to be.

*

When Rae finally finds the courage to ask, the answer comes just as she had foretold.

"No," says the ogre. "No way, no how."

She lets some days pass and asks again.

"No, Rae, no. Who'll get my tea? Who'll answer the door if someone knocks? What if your mum calls? It's Christmas soon. She'll be thinking of us now. What'll happen then?"

But she won't call, Dad, is what Rae wants to tell the poor, downtrodden ogre, but it doesn't need saying out loud. He knows it already.

Our Rae does not give up though. She may not be popular, or skilled at being free, but she's nothing short of hardworking. In all things. English, maths, housework, care. And so she applies her diligence to convincing the ogre to let her go.

It's just one day, she says, *just a few miles away*.

It's just, it's just, it's just...

And the ogre begins to soften.

He sets her tasks.

"Fix that drip on the bathroom tap, then maybe I'll let you go."

"Get the council to sort out the damp in the kitchen, then maybe I'll let you go."

"Get that Bolognese crust out of the living-room carpet once and for all, then maybe..."

So Rae wrenches and phones, she washes and scrubs. She goes above and beyond, onwards and over. She fetches paint and brushes to brighten the walls of every room, runs up a new living-room curtain to please you peerers-in. She sweeps out the kitchen cupboards, evicting all mice (which, in this story at least, show no signs of banding together to sew Rae a dress for an upcoming ball). She drags home a tree and decorates its branches, sensing a glimmer of how it might feel to sing a song in a different key. And it is only then, as the angel is placed up high, almost out of reach, that the ogre issues his final task: "Now bring back your mother."

The skin is hanging heavier than ever from the bones

of his face. His black eyes are wet in the flickering light of a late-night comedy. Laughter spills from the television.

I can't, thinks Rae. *My mother is a puff of smoke, a green gas. She was turned into a white rabbit, a pumpkin, a croaking frog, long long ago. She is far far away.*

But Rae doesn't say this. She strokes the stray hairs on the ogre's head and takes herself off to bed.

*

Morning. In the dark before dawn, while the salt winds still whistle through the alleyways and passages, Rae combs her long-long hair and decides to let it hang free. It whips across her face as she opens her bedroom window and climbs out, away from all the Thou Shalt Nots of that two-bedroomed flat above the Magical Palace. She slides down the drainpipe and waiting beneath is her Prince Ben with his trusty steed (a rust-dappled 1997 Fiat Uno he affectionately refers to as Jacob). They gallop away – just one car in a joyous family procession, off on a quest for a treasure called fun.

When they arrive in the next town, gasping exhaust smoke and their own anticipation, their mouths fall open to see a pier that hasn't slipped into the water, fairground rides that haven't been eaten by the brine. Those so-called villainous boys and witchy girls tumble out of their cars and on to the sands in search of candyfloss and a decent tattoo parlour. The rising sun dances on a clear bobbing sea, making no promises of warmth but guarantees of light. Other people arrive, and they come to play, not to sleep.

"That baby ain't mine," is what Prince Ben tells Rae later over a banquet for two – chips wrapped in paper, taken to a bench on the promenade edge. "Tanya ain't mine either."

"Oh," says Rae, fanning her mouth against the heat of a nuclear chip, a heat that comes welcome, wrapped as they are, much like their food, but in scarves and hats and jackets like duvets. The sea plays the role of the vinegar bottle, sprinkling them as each wave hits the wall. "I just do the robbing," Ben adds with a pride that doesn't seem so misplaced at the time. So when he leans in to give Rae a Tango-and-tomato-sauce kiss, I – Rae loves him back with all of her might.

*

Back home, in the thin night, Rae prepares herself for a sermon on the sinfulness of men. What she does not prepare herself for is the sight of the ogre standing at her open bedroom window.

"Go," says Rae to the prince, pushing him away. Though he knows more than her about calling up at windows and winning over the sad, he knows nothing of ogres, the way they are filled with pain, leaving no room for love.

"Are you sure?" he asks, looking up, watching as the fat, glassy tears of the ogre are whisked away by the wind.

Rae nods and the prince does as he's told, untangling his fingers from hers.

"And you can go, too," yells the ogre to his daughter. "Stay out! You're not coming back in here now you've betrayed me. The cat's got you. He can keep you. You're as bad as your evil mother."

"Shall I call the police?" These are Prince Ben's final words, but Rae shakes her head and he drives away, the sound of Jacob's engine eventually lost to the sea.

The ogre and his daughter listen to the waves sigh and swallow.

"Come out," says Rae.

"No," growls the ogre.

"Please, Dad," she says. "Let your hair down. We all need to let our hair down every once in a while."

The seagulls cry, filling her silence, and the ogre disappears from the window with a shake of his head. Rae is left alone in the wasteland of the cobbles, with the rise and fall of the sea, the cotton-wool bass of passing car stereos, the chatter and the giggle of the amusements.

But that's when the door opens, the one that leads from the street to the two-bedroomed flat above. The ogre is there – a silhouette in the yellow light that trickles down from the lobby's tired lampshade. One more step and the ogre will be out in the night, in the dangerous night, where a boy could rob him of his wallet any minute, rob him of his daughter, even. And he takes that step, the ogre, and he doesn't turn to dust, so he takes another, and another, towards the orange light of the streetlamps, towards his daughter.

Two stray passers-by twist their necks to stare at this

miraculous scene – an ogre showing itself to the world, out in real life. They turn to whisper about how he seems so much more human than they remembered. One even dares to say hello.

"Hi," replies the ogre, his voice crackling like the sound when you unwrap a parcel.

Rae takes the hand of this half man/half ogre/all father and they go, steady on the frosting cobbles, around the corner of the building to the main road, towards the excitable notes of the Magical Palace, past the boys and girls in their flammable anoraks, blowing smoke up at the artificial illuminations. And this is when the snow starts – an omen that they should go inside. So they do, Rae leading the way, towards the grab machine that promises dreams but never delivers.

"Here." She hands the ogre some gold, explains how you must press this button first, then this one, and how you only get one chance, you can't go back for more. She understands that the ogre, quivering in the newness of the air, will need directions, but she's prepared to steer him a little through the wilderness if it means she can go, every once in a while, into the undiscovered country herself.

The coin drops and the machine immediately wakes, burbling its delight. The ogre presses the first button and, as he does, Rae tells him about the wonders of the town next door, the shiny fairground, the hot fat chips. As he presses the second button, she tells him about the A-level college that's there, its impressive library.

Down drops the claw, open and ready. It closes, hungry, around … the bluebird! The bluebird! It's quite violent in a way, the sudden reflex of that grab, but so wonderful all the same. Rae grips the human skin of the ogre's wrist in anticipation as they watch the crane wobble its way back to the drop chute. She doesn't want to let go, not just yet. She wants to hold on to this moment, have it hang there in sight. Here is the promise of a 'yes', the greatest treasure of all.

But Rae does let go – because the universe has paid out! Life has delivered! The claw has opened and the bluebird is theirs! Rae jumps up and down. She claps her hands and she cheers. The machine plays a song in a key just right for a time like this. The ogre's eyes are shining, and not with tears. This Christmas won't necessarily be big and jolly, but little and merry,

Rae decides, will do. She crouches down so that she might ceremoniously collect their winnings. Here it is, a bird set free.

Routes and Wings

*

Lisa Williamson

*With thanks to members of Crisis
for sharing their stories*

I'm sitting in the windowless staffroom of Sandwich City eating the sandwich of the day (tuna melt). 'Merry Christmas Everyone' by Shakin' Stevens is crackling out of the ancient radio. It reminds me of the CD Mum used to play every year as her Christmas-present-wrapping soundtrack, singing along tunelessly, pausing every so often to swear at the Sellotape dispenser.

"Pete, can I have a word?" I ask.

Pete is my boss. He doesn't like me very much.

He groans like I've just asked him to run a marathon on my behalf.

"Fine," he says, rubbing the bridge of his nose. "Just make it quick, all right. I've got some calls to make."

Pete's always got 'calls to make'.

"It's about next week's rota," I say.

"What about it?" he asks, setting what smells like a Starbucks gingerbread latte down on the table.

Even though we get a hefty staff discount, Pete always goes elsewhere for his lunch. Today he has a brown paper bag from the burrito shop next door looped over his wrist.

"It's just that I've only got one shift. Tomorrow. Then nothing until after Christmas."

"Sorry," he says, shrugging and sounding the exact opposite. "That's the way it worked out."

"It's just that Angel has six shifts."

"She's been here longer than you," he replies, sitting down opposite me and unwrapping his jumbo-sized burrito. Even though I'm officially a veggie, it smells incredible. "She gets priority."

Nothing at all to do with the fact she has legs up to her armpits and insists on wearing an extra-small Sandwich City polo shirt, her tits permanently straining against the thin cotton material.

"She started, like, two weeks before me," I say. "*And* she's always late."

Pete glares at me, the bright yellow strip-lighting illuminating every single blackhead on his greasy nose.

Sometimes I wonder what might happen if I flirted a bit, giggled at his sexist jokes and let him 'accidentally' rub up against me behind the counter, the way Angel does. Would the rota look a bit different right now if I did?

"Are you telling me how to do my job, Lauren?" Pete asks, lowering his burrito. There's a blob of sour cream on his chin, clinging to his pathetic attempt at a beard.

I have my usual fantasy of tearing off my apron and telling him to stick his shitty job before storming out in a blaze of glory. Only I know I won't. Pete may be awful and the job may be crap, but I can't risk losing it.

"Of course I'm not telling you how to do your job," I say eventually. "I was just hoping for a few more shifts, that's all."

"You and everybody else," he says, spraying rice and refried beans with every syllable. "You have no idea how stressful it is managing you lot. No idea at all."

I take a deep breath. "Well, if anything comes up, I'm available."

"Yeah, yeah." He pauses to sip his coffee. "Was that all you wanted?" he asks.

I hesitate before nodding my head.

"Good," he says, taking out his phone and tapping at the screen with the stylus he keeps permanently tucked behind his left ear. I sigh and shovel my sandwich wrapper and empty cup into the bin.

*

My mobile vibrates against my hip as I wash my hands in the loo. I dry them off and fish out my phone from my pocket. It's an old-fashioned Nokia Milly donated after my phone got stolen.

Milly is my sort-of girlfriend. I say 'sort of' because she always acts a bit funny when I use the 'g' word – claims she doesn't like labels. I met her online before I moved down here. She's seventeen, like me, and studying hotel management at college. I smile when I see her name on the screen, but it quickly fades as I read her text.

Soz L, Mum's got the lurgy so not going out any more :(Will u be ok finding somewhere else to kip? M xx

Milly's mum doesn't like me either. Ever since she walked in on us kissing and went ballistic, she won't have me in the house. She was supposed to be out at a party tonight and Milly was going to sneak me in, then back out again in the morning while her mum slept off her inevitable hangover. I've been looking forward to it all week, every spare minute spent fantasizing about a night curled up in Milly's squishy bed, her warm body pressed against mine.

I hesitate before tapping out a short reply.

No worries. Yeah, I'll be fine. Another time? L xoxo

No reply.

*

My official job title at the Oxford Circus branch of Sandwich City is 'Sandwich Artisan'. What a laugh. As if there's any artistry involved in dolloping meatballs and slices of cheese on to a bit of bread.

There's four of us behind the counter today – Angel on the till, Tao, Stacey and I constructing the sandwiches. They're all students and either living at home or in ramshackle house shares. As far as I'm aware, they assume the same of me.

"Any joy with Pete?" Stacey asks as I pull on a fresh pair of plastic gloves and slide into the gap beside her.

"What do you think?"

She screws up her face in sympathy.

"If it's any consolation, I only have two shifts," she says. "*And* I haven't finished my Christmas shopping yet. I'm going to be soooooo skint come January."

"Tell me about it," I murmur.

"You coming tonight?" she asks.

She's talking about the Sandwich City Christmas 'do' – a meal at Pizza Express followed by drinks in Tiger Tiger; all Angel's choice from what I can gather.

I shake my head.

Stacey's face falls. "Why not?"

"Can't. Got to babysit."

"Who for?"

"My neighbour's kid. I agreed to it ages ago. I thought I mentioned it."

The lies trip off my tongue almost too easily.

"Guys," she announces to the others. "Have you heard this? Lauren's ditching us tonight to babysit!"

"What?" Angel says, pouting. "But I've booked the table for eighteen."

"Sorry," I say. "I couldn't turn it down. The money's really good."

"How good?" Tao asks, narrowing his eyes.

"Like fifteen quid an hour."

"Nice one," he says, raising his hand for a high five.

Here at Sandwich City, we're all on between four and six quid per hour, depending on our age, although I wouldn't be surprised to find out Angel gets more. As the youngest member of staff, I'm at the very bottom of the pay scale.

"Jesus," Stacey says. "I thought you lived in Harrow, not bloody Chelsea."

I shrug. "Last Saturday before Christmas, innit. They must be feeling generous."

"In that case, why are you moaning on about your shifts?" Angel asks. "You're gonna be loaded come tomorrow."

She can talk. I know for a fact her dad pays her whopper of a phone bill *and* gives her pocket money on top of what she earns here.

"It's just a one-off," I mutter, regretting making my imaginary hourly rate so high.

There's a sudden flurry of customers. By the time there's another lull, the conversation has moved on to the *X Factor* final and I'm glad.

*

"You sure you can't come out for one?" Stacey asks at the end of our shift.

Before the meal, everyone is congregating in All Bar One on Regent Street.

"Best not," I say. "I said I'd be round there by seven."

We're crammed into the tiny locker room just off the staff room getting changed out of our T-shirts and polyester trousers. Angel has just poured herself into a skintight minidress, which will probably guarantee her any shift she wants for the foreseeable future. Stacey is sniffing at her hair and frowning.

"God, I'm sick of smelling like this place," she says, sighing and spritzing it with perfume.

I shove my uniform in my locker and pull on the puffa jacket Milly lent me. It's not really my style and a bit too short on the sleeves, but it's about a hundred times warmer than the coat I had before.

"You off, then?" Stacey asks, watching me zip it up to my chin.

"Yeah," I say, heaving my backpack on to my shoulders.

She cocks her head to one side. "I've been meaning to ask you," she says. "What the hell do you keep in that thing? It always looks like it weighs a ton."

"Just stuff," I say, my voice wobbling slightly.

"What kind of stuff? Bowling balls?"

I hesitate.

"Stace is on to something," Angel chimes in, pausing from her false eyelash application. "You look like a teenage mutant ninja turtle with that thing on your back."

I laugh. It's a hollow laugh though, one with no destination.

They're both still looking at me, waiting for an explanation.

"It's just my gym kit and that," I say. I glance up at the clock to avoid making eye contact with either of them. "Shit, I'd better get off," I stammer. "Have fun tonight, yeah."

I slip out of the door with my head down before they can say anything else.

*

It's cold outside, my breath forming a little white cloud every time I exhale. I've walked maybe twenty metres when I realize I've left my gloves at the bottom of my locker. I debate going back to get them before remembering the expressions on Stacey and Angel's faces as they speculated over the contents of my overstuffed backpack. I shove my hands deep in my pockets instead and hope I won't regret my decision later.

When I first arrived in London it was summer. Light evenings and leaves on the trees, an outbreak of freckles on my face and shoulders. Now it's dark all the time and my face is permanently pale and waxy, starved of vitamin D, despite the blusher I apply from the tester pots in Boots when no one's looking.

Oxford Street is predictably packed. I wander in and out of the stuffy shops, pretending to browse. I make a list of gift recipients in my head, assigning them presents I could never afford – one of those Nespresso coffee makers for Mum, a cashmere cardigan for Nan, a pair of Nike Free trainers for Milly.

A one-way ticket back to Australia for Craig.

As I drift around Debenhams, I become aware of a security guard on my tail. I zigzag across the shop floor, just to make sure I'm not imagining it, taking sharp corners at random. I glance over my shoulder.

He's a couple of metres behind me, murmuring into his walkie-talkie. For a few seconds we eyeball each other, waiting to see who will make the next move. I want to stay, go up to the toy department and pick out an imaginary present for my baby cousin, Noah, but the dickhead security guard has sucked all the fun out of my fictional shopping spree. I give him the finger and leave by the nearest exit.

I head east up Oxford Street, before taking a left on to Tottenham Court Road, where I spend an hour mooching around the big Paperchase. I love all that stuff – notepads and pens and pencil sharpeners and rubbers and things – always have. Under my bed at home there are two ice-cream tubs crammed full of rubbers I've collected over the years – interesting ones, though, shaped like different things. My favourite looks just like a slice of watermelon – even smells like one, too. When I was little I would just sit there and sniff it for hours on end. Mum used to laugh and call me her 'little loony toon'. I wonder if they're still there or whether they've been chucked out by now. I certainly wouldn't put it past him. Craig, I mean. I picture my old bedroom stripped of my furniture and stuff, replaced with his stupid weights bench and rowing machine.

I leave Paperchase and head south down Charing Cross Road until I reach Trafalgar Square. It's packed full of tourists taking photos of the Christmas tree and listening to the carol singers gathered at its base. I weave among them, listening to their accents intermingling – Italian and Russian, Mandarin and American. I pop out on Piccadilly, near Fortnum and Mason. I've never been brave enough to go in before, intimidated by the doorman in his top hat and the fancy window displays. I enter gingerly, relieved to find it chaotic, stuffed with people searching for last-minute gifts. I head up the winding staircase to the Christmas department where I find a decoration I know Mum would just love – a turtle dove constructed from delicate white feathers. I let it dangle from my index finger as I check the price tag. Thirty quid. They must be taking the absolute piss. I notice the price of everything these days, quibbling over every last penny in my purse. Mum might even be proud if she knew.

The shops are starting to close. I head to M&M's World because it's open until midnight, watching as spoiled little kids fill up massive paper cups with sweets until they're overflowing. I check my phone. Still nothing from Milly.

Dinner is a one pound slice of pizza from a kiosk near Leicester Square station. My fingers are so cold I almost drop it. I eat it in a shop doorway, savouring every cheesy bite, saving the crust for later, wrapping it in a napkin and sticking it in my pocket. I'm thirsty, eyeing up the cans of Coke in the fridge, but daren't risk drinking anything at this stage in the night.

I walk back towards Oxford Street, dodging the tourists and clubbers. As I pass the darkened windows of Sandwich City, I picture my gloves sitting at the bottom of my locker. My fingers feel like icicles no matter how many times I point and flex them in my pockets. I expect they're all in Tiger Tiger by now, drinking sugary cocktails and dancing, Pete grinding up against Angel's round arse, his breath tickling her neck as he promises her a pay rise.

It's nearly midnight. After a quick loo break in a busy pub, I station myself at the 25 bus stop round the side of John Lewis, stamping up and down to keep the blood in my toes circulating until the driver finishes his fag and starts the engine.

The second the doors open, I fly for the back seat. Funny, when I was a little kid, I liked upstairs the best. Mum used to moan, try to persuade me to stay downstairs, but she'd always give in eventually. I'd sit at the very front where I could see everything, holding on to the bar like I was on a theme-park ride. When I first moved here, that's where I sat, my eyes as round as saucers as we passed all the stuff I'd only ever seen on the telly – The Houses of Parliament, Buckingham Palace, The Ritz – until the weather turned and I worked out the warmest spot was downstairs, above the engine. On cold nights like this, you have to move fast to stake your claim. Luckily fast is exactly what I am. I used to run the 100 metres for my school. Not good enough to train for the Olympics or anything like that, but the fastest in my year for a bit. I close my eyes for a second and imagine myself on the starting line at the county championships, strong and lean in my shorts and T-shirt. How long ago was that now? Two years? Three? I wish I could go back to that very moment, knowing what I know now. Maybe then I could change stuff, fix things. Stop Dad from running off to Spain. Stop Mum from meeting Craig. Not lose my temper the way I did. I have daydreams about it, full-on fantasies. Like, if I could have any superpower I wanted, that's what I would pick. Not flying, or invisibility, or superhuman strength. I'd want to go back in time and make everything OK again.

A few regulars get on the bus with me – the Turkish guy with kind eyes, the Irish bloke who talks to himself, the skinny woman with orange hair dragging her scuffed pink suitcase on wheels. Apart from the Turkish guy, who gives me a nod, we all pretend not to recognize one another. The Irish bloke has a bottle of wine in his hand. Even four seats away, I can smell him.

"You're a better man than you were yesterday," he announces to no one in particular, raising the bottle as if making a toast.

A girl about my age, maybe a bit older, wobbles down the aisle in her high heels before plonking herself opposite me, in the seats I can't sit in because travelling backwards makes me feel sick. She takes out her iPhone and jabs at the screen before lifting it to her ear, the dangly snowman earrings she's wearing clanking against it.

"Hey, Dad, it's me," she says in a babyish voice. "Yeah, I'm on the bus. I should get in just before one. You still OK to pick me up at the other end?"

Her dad must say 'yes' because she smiles and thanks him before hanging up.

I visualize him getting out of bed, pulling on a jumper over his pyjamas and padding downstairs to find his car keys. He'll keep the engine running while he waits, so the car is nice and warm, maybe even bring a blanket for her to drape over her knees on the short drive home.

The girl glances up from her phone and for a split second our eyes lock as she takes in my pale face, the backpack on my knee. She looks away first, wrapping the chain-link handle of her handbag round her wrist, once, twice, three times. She doesn't make a massive deal over it or anything but somehow that almost makes it worse. I want to tap her on the knee and tell her that a few months ago, I was just like her, that I wore dresses and heels and straightened my hair, too; that I used to have a nice, cosy home, just like her. I doubt she'd believe me though. Why should she?

A load of blokes dressed in Santa suits pile on at the

next stop. They're pissed, singing 'Fairytale of New York' at the tops of their voices. A couple of them clock the girl, breaking away from the rest of the group to chat her up. She seems to like it, answering their stupid questions and laughing when one of them asks if she'd like to sit on his lap. In my jeans and hoodie and Michelin Man jacket, I'm totally invisible to them. It's weird, because I used to get chatted up all the time at home. Name a cheesy chat-up line and I bet you I've heard it at least ten times before.

The bus rumbles down Oxford Street, gradually filling up until it's standing-room only. I stare out of the window as we weave our way out of the West End and through the city, past the Gherkin and St Paul's cathedral, which always puts that song from *Mary Poppins* in my head – 'Feed the Birds' – before continuing east. The journey gets boring after that. The road to Ilford, where the bus terminates, is long and straight, populated by fried chicken shops and nondescript convenience stores. Given the choice I prefer to ride the number 9, which goes through Kensington, or the 11 through Chelsea, but on nights like this, it's best to go for the longer routes to keep changes to a minimum. It means I can't play my favourite game though, the one where I pick out the houses I like the look of and fantasize about getting off the bus and opening the front door with a magic key. I've become obsessed with houses, which is funny because I was never bothered before. Whenever Mum watched Kirsty and Phil on the telly I used to get up and leave the room. Now I get the attraction. Now I understand they're more than just a loads of bricks with a roof plonked on top.

At Whitechapel, a woman gets on with her tear-stained kid, his screams drowning out the singing Santas. Poor kid, it's way past his bedtime, no wonder he's howling like that. At Bow Road, a gang of teenage boys push and shove their way up the stairs, most of them not even bothering to swipe their Oyster cards. The driver turns a blind eye, clearly not in the mood for a confrontation. I wonder if they're the ones who nicked my phone that time, back before I figured out it's not smart to sit on the upper deck after dark. They certainly look the same, with their black hoodies, furtive eyes and scarves pulled up to obscure their faces. At Stratford someone is sick on the stairs, the acidy smell of their vomit hitting my nostrils in seconds. I purse my lips together and try to block it out, burying my nose in the top of my bag.

I've seen everything on the night bus. Fist fights, drug deals, sex, break-ups, make-ups, nosebleeds, bottles smashing, screaming rows, mass singalongs, even a woman's waters breaking. And puke. So much puke.

The girl opposite me gets off at Woodgrange Park. I watch as she sprints towards the waiting car, its lights already on.

*

I wake up when my head hits the cold glass of the window with a soft thud.

Shit. I didn't mean to doze off. It's against my rules. No sleeping after dark.

I do a quick inventory, my heart beating fast as I check for my phone and wallet.

I haven't had a proper sleep for a few days now. Milly lets me kip at hers during the day sometimes, while she's at college and her mum's at work. I have to stay upstairs though, in case the neighbours spot me through the windows and tell on us. Otherwise, if I'm not at Sandwich City, I'm stuck wandering the streets. I go for miles and miles sometimes, pounding the pavements until my feet are sore. It's too cold to do anything else; I don't have the luxury of standing still any more. No wonder I've got so skinny. God, I used to love it when my jeans felt too loose. I'd wear them low on my hips like a badge of honour. Now I long for a bit of meat on my bones and everything it stands for.

Peering out of the window, I realize we're in Ilford. I check the time. 1.38 a.m. It feels later.

All change please, the automated voice says, robotic but sort of kind at the same time. I sometimes wonder who she is. An actress probably. I bet she got to sit in a cosy little recording studio somewhere, sipping tea between takes.

Reluctantly I stand up and brace myself for the ten minutes in the cold before I can climb back on again.

The Irish bloke refuses to get off. Sometimes they call the police. Tonight though, the driver clearly can't be bothered, letting him finish his bottle of wine in the relative warmth of the stationary bus while the rest of us huddle under the shelter, not speaking. The pavement is covered with a sparkling layer of frost.

I trace my toe in it, drawing a picture. It's only when I've finished, I realize I've drawn a house.

*

An hour and a half later I'm back round the side of John Lewis. Déjà vu.

I secure a seat above the engine. It's still warm from whoever was sitting in it last.

Someone gets on after me with what smells like a Maccy D's, awakening the almost permanent hollow of hunger deep in my belly. I manage to identify the telltale brown bag, relieved when its owner takes it upstairs, out of sight. It reminds me of the pizza crust in my pocket. I unwrap it, nibbling on it like a squirrel, taking tiny bites to make it last.

On automatic, I check my phone, even though I know Milly probably went to bed hours ago. 3.32 a.m. I resist yawning, knowing one will only lead to another, and another.

I don't notice her at first. I'm too busy watching a fight unfold on the pavement outside the big Primark near Tottenham Court Road station, the screams belonging to someone I assume must be one of their girlfriend's, leaking through the open door.

"Lauren?" she says.

I look up.

Angel is advancing down the aisle towards me, immaculate as always, her bare legs seemingly immune to the cold.

Shit.

That's when I remember that she lives in Stratford, right near Westfield. I curse my stupidity, my cheeks blazing as she sits down opposite me.

"I thought you were babysitting," she says, taking in the backpack on my lap, the way my arms are wrapped around it like it's the most precious thing on earth, the half-eaten pizza crust in my right hand.

"They cancelled," I say. "Got the flu."

"Where have you been, then?" she asks.

"I met up with a mate. Had a few drinks."

"You should have come to find us."

"Not really dressed for it," I say, indicating my jeans and trainers.

"Where you going now?" she asks.

"Where do you think? Home."

There's a pause.

"You do know this bus doesn't go to Harrow, don't you?" she says.

Harrow is where Milly lives. It was her address that allowed me to get the job at Sandwich City in the first place. I blink rapidly, my mind racing.

"Are you joking me?" I say. "I could have sworn it said Harrow on the display."

My voice is shaky though. I'm trying too hard.

I've always been shit at acting. I never even got a speaking part in the nativity – I would be the innkeeper's wife or one of at least a dozen mute angels, wandering aimlessly after Gabriel, wearing a halo made from silver tinsel on my head. I can't deliver a line to save my life.

Angel is looking at me, I mean, really *looking* at me, her eyes flickering as she attempts to join the dots, panic swirling in my belly with every straight line she draws.

My arm shoots out to press the bell.

Ding, ding, ding!

I pull my backpack on to my shoulders and lurch down the aisle, pressing the bell again, like that's going to make the bus reach the next stop any faster. Angel is calling my name, her heels clattering as she leaves her seat to come after me.

Shit, shit, shit.

I push the emergency door control.

"Oi!" the driver yells as the doors judder open.

I ignore him, leaping off the bus and sprinting down the nearest side street, my bag banging against my back as I run, lungs and calves on fire. Even though I know there's no chance Angel could have followed me, I don't dare stop running until I'm outside Bond Street tube station, panting hard.

I chuck myself on to the first bus I see, an N137 to Crystal Palace. The only seat left is on the top deck, right at the back. Slumped down low, I pull my hood up so all that's visible of my face is my eyes and nose. The tears that flow are red hot with shame.

*

The following morning, I brush my teeth in the loos at McDonald's, trying to ignore the curious glances of the woman washing her hands beside me.

I allowed myself to grab a bit of sleep on the bus earlier, waking up as we crossed Tower Bridge, the sun peeking over the horizon, making the River Thames glow a buttery yellow.

The girl looking back at me in the mirror has purplish half-moons under each eye, hair shiny with grease. I haven't washed it since I was last at Milly's and it shows. I yank the hood of my coat up to cover it.

*

I'm waiting outside the shop when Pete swaggers round the corner.

"You're eager," he says, fishing in his pocket for his keys, stale alcohol and chewing gum on his breath.

"My bus was early," I say.

He shrugs, obviously uninterested.

Once inside, he disappears into the cupboard-sized room he calls his office, where the phone is ringing, while I go to the locker room and change into my uniform, tucking my greasy hair into my Sandwich City cap.

When I come out, Pete's attacking the rota pinned to the corkboard on the staffroom wall with a rubber.

"Everything all right?" I ask.

"That was Angel," he says.

My heart sinks to my shoes. She's told Pete. He's removing me from the rota altogether. Reporting me to Sandwich City headquarters for passing Milly's address off as my own. I realize I'm shaking.

"Says she's woken up with the flu," Pete continues, frowning over his shoulder. "Which is funny because she seemed fine about eight hours ago."

I nod, trying to process his words alongside my last sighting of a gleamingly healthy Angel on the number 25 bus.

"Not going to be in all week apparently," he says. "Reckons I should give all her shifts to you."

I swallow hard.

"Well?" he says. "Do you want them or not?"

"Yes," I stutter. "Course I do."

"She said something about some food she left in the fridge as well," Pete adds, screwing up his face as he writes my name on the rota. "Says to have it, if you want it. Her stuff's got her name on it apparently."

I walk over to the fridge, crouching down to open the door. There's a ready meal with Angel's name printed on it in block capitals, plus a couple of yogurts, a packet of bagels, a smoothie, half a pack of blueberries. I stare at her name until the letters start to dance in front of my eyes, blurring behind a fresh film of tears.

"Since when did you two become so pally?" Pete asks, his voice thick with suspicion.

Since about 3.30 a.m. this morning, I answer silently, hugging the packet of bagels to my chest. *I just didn't realize it until now.*

About the Authors

*

Tom Becker won the Waterstones Children's Book Prize in 2007 at the age of twenty-five with his first novel, *Darkside*. As well as further books in the Darkside series, Tom has written several standalone YA horror novels, including *Dark Room* for the Red Eye series from Stripes.

Holly Bourne writes YA novels and blogs about feminist issues. Her first two books, *Soulmates* and *The Manifesto on How to Be Interesting*, have been critically acclaimed and translated into six languages. *Am I Normal Yet?* was chosen as a World Book Night book for 2016 and shortlisted for *The Bookseller* YA Book Prize.

Sita Brahmachari was the winner of the Waterstones Children's Book Prize in 2011 for her debut novel *Artichoke Hearts*. *Red Leaves* was endorsed by Amnesty International and she scripted the stage adaptation for Shaun Tan's *The Arrival*. She is Writer in Residence at Islington Centre for Refugees and Migrants.

Photo © Nadja Meister

Kevin Brooks is the author of many critically acclaimed YA books. In 2015 his novel *The Bunker Diary* was the controversial winner of the CILIP Carnegie Medal. Brooks was previously shortlisted three times for the award, with *Martyn Pig*, *The Road of the Dead* and *Black Rabbit Summer*.

Melvin Burgess won the *Guardian* Children's Fiction Award and the CILIP Carnegie Medal in 1997 for *Junk*. Another four of his novels have been shortlisted for the CILIP Carnegie Medal and in 2016 he was given a special achievement award by *The Bookseller* YA Book Prize to mark the twentieth anniversary of *Junk*'s first publication.

Katy Cannon is the author of books for teenagers and younger readers. Her YA debut, *Love, Lies and Lemon Pies* has been translated into eight languages and her forthcoming book, *And Then We Ran*, will be published by Stripes in 2017.

Cat Clarke worked as an editor and in-house writer before publishing her first novel, *Entangled*, in 2011 to critical acclaim. She is now a full-time author of gritty, gripping YA novels including *Torn*, *Undone*, *A Kiss in the Dark* and *The Lost and the Found*.

Tracy Darnton is the winning author of the Stripes YA Short Story Prize for her story 'The Letter'. She recently graduated with distinction from the Bath Spa MA Writing for Young People and is working on her debut novel.

Juno Dawson – formerly known as James – is the multi-award-winning author of dark teen thrillers *Hollow Pike, Cruel Summer, Say Her Name* and *Under My Skin*. In 2015 she released her first contemporary romance, *All of the Above*, and in 2016 she authored World Book Day title *Spot the Difference*.

Photo © Chris Gloog

Julie Mayhew is an author, playwright and actress. Her debut novel, *Red Ink,* was shortlisted for the Branford Boase Award in 2014 and her critically acclaimed second novel, *The Big Lie,* was shortlisted for Peters Book of the Year and Shropshire Teenage Book of the Year. Julie's latest novel is the Russian saga, *Mother Tongue*.

Non Pratt is author of the acclaimed *Trouble,* which was shortlisted for *The Bookseller* YA Book Prize and the Branford Boase Award, and *Remix*. After graduating from Trinity College Cambridge, she became a book editor at Usborne and now writes full-time.

Marcus Sedgwick won the Branford Boase Award in 2001 with his debut novel, *Floodland*. In 2007 *My Swordhand Is Singing* won the Booktrust Teenage Prize and in 2011 *Lunatics and Luck* won a Blue Peter Book Award. Marcus has been shortlisted for the CILIP Carnegie Medal six times.

Lisa Williamson won the Best Older Fiction category of the Waterstones Children's Book Prize in 2016 with her debut novel, *The Art of Being Normal*. It was also shortlisted for *The Bookseller* YA Book Prize and the Brandford Boase Award and was the bestselling YA hardback debut of 2015.

Benjamin Zephaniah is an internationally renowned performance poet and acclaimed author of bestselling YA novels *Face*, *Gangsta Rap*, *Teacher's Dead*, *Refugee Boy* and *Terror Kid*. He has inspired a generation of rappers and performance poets and has been awarded sixteen honorary doctorates in recognition of his work.

About the Illustrator

William Grill is a freelance author/illustrator based in London. He has worked for a variety of clients such as *The New York Times*, Radley, Harrods and Shelter. His debut book *Shackleton's Journey* won the CILIP Kate Greenaway Medal and has been translated into over fourteen languages.

"If you can't do away with all your prejudices at Christmas, if you cannot suspend your disbelief, and you can't work together for something like homelessness, then there's not much chance for society."
– Crisis founder Bill Shearman

Christmas can be an incredibly difficult time of year for a person cut off from family and home. One in four homeless people spends Christmas alone.

Crisis at Christmas offers support, companionship and vital services and the chance for homeless people to take up the life-changing opportunities on offer all year round at centres run by Crisis across the country.

In 2015 volunteers in London, Newcastle, Edinburgh, Birmingham and Coventry donated their time to cut hair, lead karaoke sessions, scrub potatoes, perform medical examinations or just have a cup of tea and a chat. Dentists, counsellors, podiatrists and massage therapists all lent their skills to help make homeless guests feel special.

Things have come a long way since Crisis was founded in December 1967, when prospective Conservative Party candidate Bill Shearman joined forces with a network of homelessness service providers and social activists working to raise awareness of homelessness and destitution in East London.

Backed by the groundswell of public support following the BBC film *Cathy Come Home,* Shearman enlisted Shadow Chancellor Iain Macleod to launch an awareness raising appeal, leading to a candle-lit vigil in Hyde Park attended by 3,000 people. By 1971, a small team of volunteers began to provide food and shelter for homeless people at the first 'Open Christmas' in an East London church.

In the intervening years the event grew in scale and ambition. Crisis at Christmas is now run by the national homelessness charity Crisis, which offers year-round services and campaigns to help end homelessness in the UK.

Last year over 4,000 people came to Crisis at Christmas, looked after by 10,000 volunteers. Tens of thousands more donated money and materials to help make the event happen.

By buying this book, you too are helping the homeless people who come to Crisis this Christmas. You are responding to the challenge laid out by Bill Shearman. You are proof that there is hope for society.

To donate, volunteer or campaign for Crisis, visit **www.crisis.org.uk**

Registered Charity Numbers:
E&W1082947, SC040094.

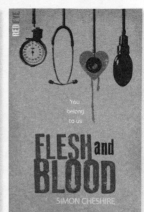

The YA Book Prize is the only book prize for YA fiction written by authors based in the UK and Ireland. Launched by *The Bookseller* magazine in 2014, the prize was created to promote the fantastic books for teenagers and young adults that are being published today.

The prize was a huge hit with publishers and readers alike, and was in 2016 awarded to *One* by Sarah Crossan, a free verse novel about conjoined twins Tippi and Grace, at the Hay Festival.

More information is available online at:

thebookseller.com/ya-book-prize/2016